BAD ORDER

BAD ORDER

A Little Known Tale of
REGULAR KIDS and HOLOGRAPHIC ALIENS
Facing an INTERDIMENSIONAL CATASTROPHE

BY B. B. ULLMAN

STERLING CHILDREN'S BOOKS
New York

For the girls in Twin Falls Middle School Book Club who read *Bad Order* when it was a struggling manuscript. Thank you, Paula, Juliana, Bella, Adriana, and Caroline for your enthusiasm, good sense, and humor.

—B.U.

STERLING CHILDREN'S BOOKS
New York

An Imprint of Sterling Publishing Co., Inc.
1166 Avenue of the Americas
New York, NY 10036

ISBN 978-1-4549-3106-5

Library of Congress Cataloging-in-Publication Data

Names: Ullman, Barb Bentler, author.
Title: Bad order : a little known tale of regular kids and holographic
  aliens facing an interdimensional catastrophe / by B.B. Ullman.
Description: New York, NY : Sterling Publishing Co., Inc., [2019] | Summary:
  Mary Day, her mute, telepathic brother, Albie, friend Brit and her brother
  Lars learn there is a leak in the dimensional universe and unless Albie
  repairs it, evil thoughts will take over.
Identifiers: LCCN 2019005914 (print) | LCCN 2019007981 (ebook) | ISBN
  9781454935360 (E-Publication/EPUB) | ISBN 9781454931065 (hardback)
Subjects: | CYAC: Brothers and sisters—Fiction. | Selective mutism—Fiction.
  | Telepathy—Fiction. | Friendship—Fiction. | Extraterrestrial
  beings—Fiction. | Science fiction. | BISAC: JUVENILE FICTION / Science
  Fiction. | JUVENILE FICTION / Visionary & Metaphysical. | JUVENILE FICTION
  / Action & Adventure / General.
Classification: LCC PZ7.U335 (ebook) | LCC PZ7.U335 Bad 2019 (print) | DDC
  [Fic]—dc23
LC record available at https://urldefense.proofpoint.com

Distributed in Canada by Sterling Publishing Co., Inc.
c/o Canadian Manda Group, 664 Annette Street
Toronto, Ontario M6S 2C8, Canada
Distributed in the United Kingdom by GMC Distribution Services
Castle Place, 166 High Street, Lewes, East Sussex BN7 1XU, England
Distributed in Australia by NewSouth Books
University of New South Wales, Sydney, NSW 2052, Australia

For information about custom editions, special sales, and premium and corporate purchases,
please contact Sterling Special Sales at 800-805-5489 or
specialsales@sterlingpublishing.com.

Manufactured in Canada

Lot #:
2 4 6 8 10 9 7 5 3 1
04/19

sterlingpublishing.com

Cover design and interior design by Irene Vandervoort

BAD ORDER

Thoughts from baby Albert . . .

In his thoughts he called her Pearl, though her name was Mary. She was different from everyone else because she understood him. With Pearl, Albert didn't have to struggle with translations or speech or gestures. He could just do what came naturally, which meant sending memos. And Pearl could read them.

Albert saw at once what a steady, good spirit she was, and he also saw that she comprehended his messages with the ease and intuition of a very advanced mind. When Albert realized this, he sent her a memo filled with awe and affection, showing Pearl a portrait of herself as she really was: a girl like a pearl of infinite value, glowing in a vast universe, here on this blue planet, here in this small house, born into this family, *his* family. Surely, she was the best sister in the world.

1
Mary and the visitors

I hadn't wanted a brother. I hadn't wanted Ma to go to the hospital. I hadn't wanted Meemaw to come over and babysit me. But I was only five, so what could I do? I could go around sulking, only that got boring. Plus, it was a waste of energy because Meemaw would only ignore me and watch TV. And anyhow, Meemaw turned out to be sort of interesting—the way she would talk to me with bad words and all, like how she would talk to any adult.

"You look like you just stepped in a big ole cow pie." That was Meemaw being sympathetic after Ma brought the new baby home. "Babies are a pain in the rear, but you'll get used

3

to him. He's a dumb, stinky baby, and you're a smart five-year-old." Meemaw gave me a head-nod like a cocky rooster. "To baby Albert you are cool as a cucumber—practically a teenager."

Meemaw's sharp wisdom *did* make me feel better.

On the third day of the new baby, Meemaw and I were eating pudding cups and watching a TV show that I didn't understand; it was all dramatic with silly adults messing up their lives. The new baby was sleeping in his cradle next to Meemaw's recliner. Ma was resting in her bedroom down the hall.

Meemaw began to doze. I think I may have been dozing, too.

I jumped. There'd been a *tap-tap-tap* on the front door; the careful knock of a visitor who didn't want to disturb. I looked over at Meemaw in her recliner. Her head was thrown back and her exhales were *shnooshling* and gurgling like a coffee maker.

Tap-tap-tap.

I got up and opened the door. *Brr.* It was cold and snowy outside.

There were three people standing on the porch—a tall lady with very shiny, yellow hair—a medium height, black man with a skin-close buzz cut—and a small, pale man; almost as pale as the deepening snow. All three of them wore black suits and goggly, brown-tinted glasses.

"Hello," said the pale man. He was bald as a melon. "We hear you have a new addition to the family." He grinned and glanced at the cradle next to Meemaw. His smile showed teeth like square, beige tiles. The television talked about cleaning your floor.

"Meemaw, there's some guys at the door." I figured I'd hand this over to an adult.

Meemaw continued making coffee. "*Shnooshle*," she uttered from dreamland.

I stared up at the tall lady. She was like a giant, but probably that was because I was very small.

"We do not wish to disturb," the pale man said. "Here is a pamphlet for the infant to read."

"Huh?" I said.

"The triad sends greetings and trifles," he added.

I had no idea what a triad was—or a trifle, for that matter. It was with reluctance that I reached out and took the pamphlet. When I did, the pale man nudged a fabric bag forward with his foot, and peeking out of the top of the bag was a little stuffed lamb. The man bobbed his head and gave me a strangely disconnected smile. When I think back on it, it was like a cartoon copy of a smile, with a row of teeth clicking softly in a face that didn't seem to cooperate.

The pale man took a step backward, and the other two followed his lead. They stood in a line, tall to short, and they all smiled that cartoon smile. Next, they raised their arms at the elbow to give me a four-fingered wave—like how little kids do. "Goodbye," they all said in unison. They turned as one and tiptoed off the front porch.

I watched the three suits glide away through the snow, and I shivered, partly because I was cold, and partly because there was something very odd about those guys. I picked up the gift bag and shut the door—and locked it.

"*Shnooshle...*" Meemaw murmured again, still fast asleep.

I snatched the white lamb out of the bag. It was so sweet with silky soft curls and a green satin ribbon, really more appropriate for a little girl than a baby—when all of a sudden Albert woke up. His eyes were wide and he made a sound like a kitten. Swaddled in pale blankets and snug in his wooden cradle, Albert was watching me like his brown eyes had tractor beams.

Ma had told me on the phone when they were still in the hospital that they were spending extra time there for observation because Albert stared so much, and cried so little. Yeah, he was good at staring, that was for sure.

I meant to take the lamb, but I feared that Albert would know I was stealing from him and I guess I didn't want him to know I could be bad like that. So I traded. I gave him the pamphlet instead.

"Look, Albert, see the pretty picture?" I held the pamphlet for him to see, and I put the lamb behind my back. Albert stared and stared at the paper, which had a bunch of stars on it. He found it so interesting that I took another look at it, too. There were some letters that made some words, only I couldn't read yet. There were dots and symbols and numbers. I recognized *e* and *x*. I remember 0 and 1, but most of it was just clutter in my head.

"Here, you keep the picture," I said, and I propped it up in his cradle.

Albert stared and stared at that pamphlet.

I backed out of the living room and ran to my tiny bedroom down the hall. I threw myself on the bed and scrunched the lamb under my pillow. I would hide it, and it would be all mine. I deserved a gift for being a good girl and not crying when Ma brought the baby home. It occurred to me that no one thought to bring a gift for little Mary—only for the cute new *baby*. Sad tears leaked out of my eyes and I used the lamb to wipe them away. Oh, I felt sorry for myself. My world was so changed, so rotten and—WHAT?

I sat up and looked around. It wasn't like I'd heard a sound with my ears, but there was something . . .

"Hello?" I said out loud.

It was a message—a message that came into my brain. And it was from Albert. He hadn't squawked or cried or talked. It was another kind of communication, like a combo of pictures and stuff that took shape in my head, like a thought bubble from a comic strip, only it melted into places where I could figure it out. I don't know how I knew it was from Albert—I just knew.

He was telling me that he really liked the pamphlet, and the way he told me was that he put a picture in my head of twinkling stars in a really cool pattern. *Pretty order* was how I interpreted it; at least those were the words that came into my brain after the message made itself known. Plus, surprise!—Albert liked me . . . a lot. A new message appeared, showing a radiant pearl in a vast space of soft, velvety green. The feelings that flowed from the pearl were kindness, and patience, and tolerance. I could feel its beauty and gigantic value, and all of a sudden I knew exactly what Albert was saying without a word: *I* was the pearl. I was like a fantastic, one-in-a-bazillion-person, and then and there, he nicknamed me Pearl. In a voice that was part of the picture, he said, **Hi, Pearl. You are the best sister ever.**

Well, that changed everything.

2
THE TRIAD SENDS GREETINGS

The Commodore was a smart-mass-holograph-research unit sent with his counterparts to collect and transmit data. Though he'd named himself the Commodore, he was actually 112000x (first unit of his triad). His solid-mass identity emerged as absurd and ironic in his estimation and it tickled his logic sequences immensely. He had learned *humor* thirty-three Earth-years ago; thus, his little bald head and strange black suit, and even his chosen designation as the Commodore made him want to vocalize the spasms called laughter. It all belied the staggering power of the triad and its colossal capacity for data.

With time, he and his counterparts 113000x and 114000x had merged into a very effective triad. They had become the Commodore, Med Tech Tek, and Citizen Lady. Together they sent back more data than any ten-thousand SMHR units in the field.

When deemed necessary, they would alter their names and speak the language that coincided with relative cultural surroundings, but their schematic appearance remained the same—mostly because Med Tech Tek had written the program as an approximate humanoid schematic and he never did fine-tune the thing, and what's more, he didn't care to. (There were far more interesting things to pursue with their time.) Of course the Commodore knew that when they went solid-mass their appearance was less than perfection (he could detect skepticism in the countenance of observers). Med Tech Tek really should fix the program, or he—the Commodore—should adjust the thing. Citizen Lady was generally immersed in research and development . . . So alas, the triad simply never got around to dealing with that particular task.

Data collection and transmission had been routine until the Extraordinary Mind arrived on the scene. The Commodore couldn't help himself. He was drawn in by *curiosity*—which he had learned seventy-one Earth-years ago. This Mind conducted itself in a very civilized manner, making polite inquiries forthwith. So impressed was the Commodore that he and his counterparts made a physical visit to the primitive dwelling on Earth's surface.

Upon closer contact, the Commodore realized that the Mind was an indigenous infant whose very existence was a marvel of genetics and happenstance. The Commodore gifted the infant with a universal smart-mass-holograph encyclopedia, and then he and his counterparts promised to keep in touch with the Mind, who called itself Albert. They made traditional gestures of departure to the exemplary one called Pearl, and they left, excitedly communicating their estimations of the situation. The Commodore experienced a vibration of extreme satisfaction over meeting that boy— dare he call the buoyant surge… *happiness*? Yes, that seemed entirely appropriate. The Commodore learned happiness, then and there.

3
Eight years later . . .

The power lines only buzzed like that when it was snowing. I scrunched my pillow into a better shape and smiled. No school today. No school tomorrow. It was winter break—sweet! I checked the clock—and there was Albert standing next to my bed looking all sleepy in his *Star Wars* jammies. His baby face was dark and serious under a mop of messy black hair. He was staring intently at my alarm clock (with a booger in his nose and his shirt inside out).

"It's not going to ring, Albie. I'm on winter break."

Albert just stared at the clock. I didn't expect him to look at me. Most of the time, eye contact gave Albert the creeps. He claimed that eyes distracted him from his brain movie. I really didn't get it.

"If you go blow your nose, you can come in the blanket cave." He liked the blanket cave because he could think about stuff *in the warmth and quiet of Pearl*—that was his thought, not mine.

Albert pattered to the bathroom and blew his nose. Then he hurried back and climbed in my bed, lying there still as a statue.

I thought about calling Brit to see if she could come over. Maybe she could bring her good sled and we could try making a run on the power-line hill, or we could build a hitchhiking snowman down on Kelly Road; that would be funny.

"Albie, you wanna come with me and Brit and play in the snow?" Albert could go either way when it came to playing outside, but if he committed, I knew I could count on him to be a good sport. He rarely complained—and for sure never out loud.

My question about playing in the snow broke the spell of the blanket cave. Albert shot out of bed and ran off. Goofy little guy. I heard him banging around in Ma's room. Actually, it was both their rooms. Ma had put a wall of bookcases down the middle, so they each got half; bummer for them that they had to share a room. But it enabled everyone to get a little bit of private space. Poor Meemaw had to sleep in the laundry room! This always cracked me up because it sounded so much worse than it was. True, she had to live with the washer and dryer and the water heater, but there was also a nice day bed and a dresser, and her little TV. *And* she could slip out to the back porch and smoke her ciggies whenever she wanted. Because of Meemaw, the laundry at our house was always done and folded.

"Jane, you want coffee?"

It was Meemaw in the kitchen talking to Ma.

"What do *you* think," Ma joked. They both loved their coffee. I had learned to make it the way Ma liked so I could bring her a cup now and then.

"Mary, you up?" Meemaw called.

"Yeah."

"You want a pancake?"

"Yeah, in a bit."

I got out of bed and went to the window. There was a lot of snow out there. When I refocused, I saw myself in the glass: a happy girl with a wide smile, a short nose, and nice brown eyes. My hair was dark like my brother's, only mine was straight—not curly like his. I ran a hand over my forehead. *Eww*—my bangs were on the verge of being oily, but I'd be wearing a hat, so no biggie. I blew out some breath and the happy girl vanished in the fog. I touched my finger to the cold glass and drew a happy face. "Walking in a winter wonderland," I sang quietly.

I was thinking that Brit could probably walk up here in twenty minutes if she couldn't get a ride. Or maybe Ma would go pick her up if the snowplow had—I suddenly got a flash of a thought. It was like a lightning strike, only the lightning was red. The startling memo stabbed at my nerves and sent a feeling through my body, and the words for the feeling were **bad order**; jarring, sickening, bad order. For some reason, it made the hairs on my neck tickle—and not in a good way.

4
Snow day

I yelled down the hall. "Albert, are you okay?"

Ma and Meemaw believed that our communication was mostly a game since Albert never said anything. I think they liked the idea that I included him in everyday stuff, and that was good enough.

Albert responded with a memo that claimed interest in the snow; something about **frozen crystals gathering**. He sent pictures of snowflakes, along with a sense of teeth-chattering cold—but it was grim and fake. Albert was a terrible liar.

I crossed the hall and checked in on him. He was in his closet where he'd been rummaging for snow clothes. A pile of cold-weather gear was heaped on the floor next to him.

"What was that lightning thing you sent me?" I asked. "And what's"—I lowered my voice to a whisper—"what's 'bad order'?"

Albert didn't look at me. His memo said **Oops, mistake?** with a silly question mark that wriggled.

"Really?" I said.

He blinked **Oops, mistake?** a few more times, but the icky feeling lingered. A sense of dread accompanied **Oops, mistake?** and I couldn't seem to shake it.

Yeah. He was lying, all right.

I waited a long time for Brit. She had to walk up from Honey Park because her mom wouldn't drive, and my mom wouldn't go out until the streets were plowed—plus Brit had to find her snow clothes and then dig the sled out of their gross garage.

Honey Park sounds all nice, but really, it was a lousy neighborhood with old houses that had once been summer cottages. The poor old cottages kept getting shabbier and uglier, and bit by bit, trailers began to replace the decrepit cabins. The trailers would get parked on the lots and hooked into utilities, while the original dwellings fell apart. Brit's house was still a house, but it was pretty run-down. And her neighbors were weird; the police were always showing up because there were fights and drugs and stuff. No one was proud to say they lived at Honey Park, even though it had a nice-sounding name.

Our house was at the end of Myrtle Road at the gravel

turnaround. If the road were paved, I suppose you would call it a cul-de-sac—but it wasn't, so it was just a dead end. Our neighborhood was nicer than Honey Park, though not by much. It was as if all the homeowners were too tired or too busy working or too poor to make their houses cuter. I guess *we* had moved out here because it was way cheaper than in the city, where my dad was getting his degrees. He was super smart, only we didn't have much money, so when my parents found this house on Myrtle, they went for it.

Brit finally got to my house, and we decided we should have sandwiches before heading out because, as usual, Brit hadn't eaten. Now we were broiling in the living room, putting our gloves and boots back on.

Albert appeared in shiny snow pants with a Goodwill snowboard hat that had brown, furry ears hanging down—they were supposed to look like hound dog ears. Meemaw was standing behind him, straight-faced. "Guess your brother wants to come, too."

"I said he could," I confirmed.

"Jane, do you mind if Albert goes out with the girls?" Meemaw called to Ma.

Ma was in the kitchen washing the dishes. She didn't have to work that week because she was a secretary for the school district. She was on winter break, just like me.

"Keep an eye on him, Mary," Ma called back.

"*Duh*," I said, zipping up my jacket.

Ma poked her head into the living room. "Would you quit with the *duh* business?"

"Sorry, I guess it's a bad habit."

"*Duh*," she said.

Brit and I checked each other for a mutual smirk, and then the three of us ventured out into a good six inches of snow. We hiked around the house, through the backyard, and past the garage where my dad used to have his lab. It was still locked up tight, which was dumb because we needed the space. But Ma left it like that, and Meemaw let her call the shots.

It had quit snowing and the air was clean and quiet. I sniffed a lungful of cold air through my nose and my nostril hairs froze. Our boots made a satisfying *scrunchy-squeak* sound as we walked.

I liked the way the snow transformed things; you couldn't see our tacky roof patch, and even the garbage cans looked picturesque, topped with dollops of snow, like big cupcakes. The borders that defined our yard and the walkway and the road were just . . . gone. The snow hugged it all and rolled on, clean and quiet.

Behind our garage was a trail that led to the power lines;

for a while it paralleled Mr. Shinn's electric fence. His house was up by the road, but back here the fence line followed the edge of his rocky goat field. We passed one of his sagging sheds, and even that looked pretty in the snow.

All us kids were scared of grouchy old Mr. Shinn *and* his fence. Rumor had it that the fence was so electrified it would kill a goat, but I think somebody made that up. I touched it once and it didn't kill me.

"Albert, don't touch the fence, it's electric." I knew that he knew this, but it made me feel better to say it in case he was getting spacey—which he was. "Albert?" He had slowed down to a shuffle back a ways, and he kept flipping the silly ears on his hat to look at the garage.

"Come on, Albie, you gotta keep up."

He picked up his pace, but then he slowed down again, twisting the ears to stare into the woods. He sent me a memo that implied interest in the snowy scene, only something else leaked through. It was **bad order** again.

5
Crazy crow

There was an ominous pause after that memo, and then the silence was broken with the noise of flapping and cawing—a crazy crow was hurtling through the woods and aiming right at Albert. It swooped down on him as if to attack. I grabbed a stick and ran back to meet it. "Go away!" I yelled, whacking the trees around me in an effort to frighten the bird.

Brit was close behind me throwing snowballs at the crow. With her good aim, she managed to nail him right on the noggin. Albert was crouching low as the bird flapped above him. It jerked this way and that way in wild-eyed confusion. And then it took off. We watched it zigzag into the forest, a beautiful black bird flying into the frosty white landscape. It called out one more resounding cry that seemed almost . . . sad.

Brit's eyes were huge. "What the hay?" she exclaimed.

We hurried out of the woods and onto the power-line road. Albert still hadn't bothered to send me a memo that could explain the strange behavior of the crow, and he was usually able to tune into animals really well. Finally I just asked him, "Albert, what happened back there? Did you do something to bug that crow?"

No teasing of crows! Albert's memo was indignant. He reminded me how much he liked crows by showing me a picture of a flying black bird with a pretty presentation of feathers around it.

"Then why was it acting so crazy?"

This time he sent me a solid and serious question mark, along with the words **More information is needed.**

"You can give me your opinion at least."

He responded with a careful memo that was cushy and soft. **No worries for Pearl. More information is needed.**

"What's going on?" Brit asked. She was used to me having these one-sided conversations.

"*Grr.* Albert won't tell me what happened back there. He just says he needs more information and he doesn't want me to worry."

Brit shoved her gloved hands in her pockets. "That bird acted like it was threatened. Maybe it was just protecting its territory or something."

"Maybe," I said, unconvinced.

Brit started pulling the sled again. "Mary, he'll tell you when he figures it out—right, Albert? Come on, let's forget about it for now and have a good time."

She was right. Christmas break was almost over, but we had snow, and we had a sled, and we had each other to goof around with. "Okay." I grinned. "Onward!" I started marching with exaggerated enthusiasm.

It *was* really pretty out here. No one had messed up the snow yet. It was a smooth, white blanket in every direction. Above us, the pearly clouds hung low and the power lines crackled.

"We are the first people in this snowy land!" Brit yelled dramatically. She waved her red scarf and started running, so Albert and I chased her.

Brit and I got along really well, plus she didn't mind Albert tagging along. She was used to him because she practically lived at our house. Her mom was okay when she was sober, but Mrs. Stickle definitely had her ups and downs—which made Brit's home life unpredictable. Despite all that, Brit was a steady person. She'd always gotten super good grades, and most of all she was nice, and I liked nice people.

When Brit hit eighth grade, she shot up and got tall and skinny. Since her name was Brit Stickle, someone started calling her "Stick Brickle," and it really caught on. I knew she hated it; it made her feel like a doofus . . . that and being hit hard with acne and zero hope of a dermatologist because her family didn't have insurance. Plus she didn't have much variety in the stuff she wore because she just didn't have a lot of clothes. But jeans and hoodies were practically the uniform at our school, so I thought she fit in fine.

When Brit got bummed about this stuff, I'd remind her that it was just a phase, that she would end up gorgeous and brilliant, which was what she really was. I mean, she was smart. If she hadn't been so shy, for sure she would have been captain of the Equationauts, which was our math team at Adeline Dillmore Middle School. We were the Dillmore Snapping Turtles. Could they have thought of a dumber mascot?

One day when she was feeling super-low, I told her, "Brit, you are going to look back on all this and just laugh. You are so much smarter and nicer and prettier than anyone in this whole school."

"Right. Too bad *they* don't know it." Her face was sullen and kind of angry when she said this, but I knew Brit too well. Tears were not far away.

"Of course they don't know it," I said, keeping my face serious. "Those dumb Snapping Turtles couldn't find their butts in a blizzard."

Brit recognized the phrase as something Meemaw might

say. "Your Meemaw is having a bad influence on you." She shook her head but managed a smile.

The snow was too deep for good sledding, so we kept on walking to Kelly Road. There, we found a hill where the snow had been compacted, and we pig-piled to take a test run. It was really fast and we had a spectacular wipeout at the bottom.

"Car!" Brit called.

We got off the road for the approaching vehicle.

"I hope it's not anyone we know," Brit said. "We look sorta dorky sledding like kids."

"We sorta *are* kids," I reminded her.

"No, we're teenagers," she said—and she didn't sound thrilled.

Brit and I had turned thirteen back in August. We had celebrated a double birthday, just like we'd done for years. We liked it that way. It was way more festive.

"Whew, it's just Lars," Brit said, grinning at the slow-moving truck. Lars was Brit's older brother. He looked a lot like her: pale and blonde and skinny, only he'd gotten through that awkward phase that Brit was in now. He'd ended up cute in a lean, intense sort of way.

Lars Stickle was in his sophomore year and he ran with

a tough crowd. He worked at the Honest Lube changing people's oil and had saved enough money to buy a crappy pickup truck. It was a patchwork of parts and primer and it left a cloud of blue smoke everywhere it went.

I gave Lars a halfhearted wave—then a snowball soared through the air and exploded on the driver's side window. Brit had thrown it, and she was laughing and running for cover, so I ran, too, dragging Albert with me.

Lars and his coworker, Tim Guthrie, leapt out of the truck, throwing snowballs as they pursued us. They got us good, and I took a snowball in the ear. I appreciated that they didn't target Albert.

"Okay, okay!" Brit cried. "Truce!"

Lars was laughing at the easy triumph, but he seemed happy to quit the game—he didn't have gloves on. "That'll teach you little rug-gnats," he said with a smug grin. "Not a bad shot, Brit," he added.

She beamed at the compliment.

"Me and Tim are going over to Pacco's to practice," he informed her. Lars was in a band with Tim, and Pacco Morrison, and Pacco's brother Mike. The band was called Gut Me, so yeah, it was pretty bad . . . though Gut Me did a battle-of-the-bands at the high school and people hadn't booed. That was something, anyway. Lars was actually good on the guitar when he wasn't banging out ear-splitting chords.

Lars said, "Mom's a little out of it today."

Brit lost her smile. "She must be getting a start on New Year's."

"I was going ask you to sleep over," I said quickly.

Lars gave me a tiny nod. "I can swing by with your toothbrush and stuff," he offered. "You want your old bear? What's her name—Douchey?"

"Quit calling her Douchey!" Brit smacked Lars on the arm. "She's *Darcy* and she helps me sleep."

The two boys returned to the truck, snickering. From the still-open window Lars gave Brit a wave that was just him pointing his finger at her—she nodded back. The pickup roared up the hill, leaving a cloud of smoke in the air and a dirty spot on the snow.

Albert wasn't one to smile or get too excited, but he definitely had a sparkle in his eyes that afternoon. When we pig-piled for the last run, I knew he was happy. He sent me a nice memo; something about cold and acceleration, but also about **the good company of Pearl and Equationaut**. Ever since Brit joined the math team, she'd become "Equationaut" in Albert's memos. This never failed to crack me up.

We crossed our footprints on the power-line road, hiking back the way we had come. The clouds had turned heavy and steely gray, and the twilight was painting the snow a cold blue. Feathery flakes started falling again, and the electric lines buzzed like crazy. After we turned onto the Shinn trail, it all went quiet, protected from the noisy buzz by a wall of trees. We marched single file next to Mr. Shinn's electric fence, careful to keep our distance. I kept looking warily into the woods. "Do you think it's still around—the crow I mean?"

"I doubt it." Brit was behind me, dragging the sled. "I don't think they're active after the sun goes down."

I checked on Albert. He was way behind Brit, moving slower and slower; he was staring at the woods again.

"Albert, what are you looking at?"

I scanned the trees and bushes. It was just a quiet forest, made quieter by the drifting snow. "The crow went to bed, Albie." My breath came out in frosty clouds and lingered with the moment. I couldn't see anything that looked particularly interesting—evergreens, a fallen tree, six old posts where I guess a shed used to be—all covered by a layer of snow that had managed to filter down through the branches. What was he looking at? You just never knew with Albert.

"Come on, Albie, it's getting dark and my feet are freezing."

I waited for Albert to slowly catch up and then I took his hand to get him moving, but he stopped and yanked it away.

Once again he was staring as if hypnotized by the shadowy woods.

Brit had passed me on the trail, but now she backtracked to see what was holding us up. "What are you guys looking at?"

"I don't know—Albert sees something."

6
Another weird thing

I followed my brother's gaze, straining my eyes in the fading light. The tree silhouettes looked purple now and the tops of the old posts held tall slices of snow. Nothing moved. But then I saw something. "Do you see a reddish mist over there?" I asked. "Look in the middle of those posts—it's more visible if you don't look right at it."

"Oh, yeah, I see it." Brit squinted. "Like somebody exhaled and their breath came out red."

I shivered. There was something wrong with the mist. I felt like maybe we should get the heck out of there. At that moment Albert confirmed my uneasiness with a red memo that said **Danger**.

"Hey, you kids!" A gravelly voice came from behind us. When I turned around, a light blinded me; I couldn't see past the glare. "You better watch it, messin' around in these woods. It ain't safe."

It sounded like old Mr. Shinn. He kept pointing the flashlight right in my face. "Something might *gitcha*," he said.

"We're not on your property!" Brit snapped. "Mrs. Day owns all this—all the way to the power lines." Wow, Brit's natural shyness took a back seat when she had to stick up for somebody else.

Mr. Shinn pointed his flashlight at Brit and away from me, so my eyes had time to adjust. I could see him, now, on the other side of the fence in his ratty overcoat and a dirty, plaid hat with earflaps.

"I'm glad it *ain't* my property," he grumbled. "Just sayin' you better steer clear 'lest you're looking for trouble with a capital *T*."

He was holding something in his other hand. Something shaped like a gun. Turning abruptly, the old man ambled away across his snowy field. I watched the wobbling beam of his flashlight until I couldn't see it anymore.

"Well, that was weird," I said.

"What a creeper!" Brit exclaimed.

Albert sent no comment.

I tried to focus again on the faint, red fog. "What *is* that stuff, Albert?"

Albert took my hand, which wasn't like him; he rarely initiated touch of any kind. He only tolerated the sledding

31

because he was on top and he liked going fast. But now he scooted ahead of me and gave me a tug. He even pushed Brit to get her moving. He sent me no explanation at all.

When we reached the backyard, I breathed a sigh of relief. In the swirling snowfall the house looked super cozy with cheerful, yellow windows and smoke puffing out of the chimney. Our house was beautiful.

"Hey Mary, check it out—a coyote." Brit tipped her head at the dog-like animal slinking out of the woods behind us. It stopped when we stopped and crouched low in the snow.

For the second time, Albert tugged my hand to get me moving.

"It's okay, Albert; they're scared of people. He must be hungry to come so close. Good thing we don't have a cat, right, Brit?" Brit and I had a joke about LOST CAT signs around Myrtle Road—that they ought to say, GOODBYE, DEAR FLUFFY because we always figured the coyotes got them.

The coyote was at the edge of the garage, watching us. This was odd; normally they were such careful and shy creatures and they'd skitter off before your eyes could even track them. But this one stayed. And it growled.

"Oh my God, could this day get any weirder?" Brit threw a snowball at the coyote. "Get lost!" she said harshly.

Instead of slinking off, the creature came nearer, making a guttural sound. My heart skipped with a thud. This wasn't right. I stepped in front of Albert.

"Run to the porch," I ordered.

At that moment, an immense shadow took shape from above. A pale bird swooped silently down and landed on the coyote, talons outstretched. It was a huge owl, and it clawed and pecked at the neck of the coyote, while the shocked coyote snarled and snapped its jaws, twisting to free itself. And then from nowhere, a crow descended to join the skirmish, tormenting both the owl and the coyote.

"Mary, move!" Brit shouted. I'd been mesmerized, watching the bizarre show. We all bumbled up the back porch steps and burst into Meemaw's room. I watched through the window as the coyote freed itself and ran. The owl and crow continued to spar in a cyclone of combat until they separated and flew into the snowy night.

"What the hay?" Brit was looking at me with her eyebrows arched high in alarm.

"Do you think it was the same crazy crow?" I asked.

Albert memoed a grim **YES**.

We spilled our story about the coyote and the birds as we hung our wet snow clothes on chairs by the woodstove. Ma and

Meemaw were setting the table, and they didn't know what to think about the strange nature show we described. Finally Meemaw said, "I'll bet they were after the compost. I tossed the leftover pancakes in there this morning. I s'pose the food could have gotten 'em all riled. I do make good pancakes," she added.

"I didn't think of that! We were standing right next to the compost. Maybe that's what they were fighting over." This explanation made me feel so much better; it was logical and grounded in everyday stuff. Even if it didn't exactly explain the behavior of the crow on the trail, it had such a sensible tone.

7
Old turd on toast

We all gathered in the dining room to have stew and biscuits that Ma had made from scratch. She'd lit some candles on the table and the room felt warm and snug. Our wet snow gear was steaming by the woodstove, lending a damp-fabric smell to the house.

"And another weird thing," I blurted. "We ran into Mr. Shinn on the trail and he was acting even more creepy than usual."

"That man is a pain in the rear," Meemaw grumbled. "Jane, remember when I tried to get him to help you with your car? He wouldn't lift a finger—and you, a widow. Ed Shinn is an old turd on toast." Meemaw was shaking her head in disgust.

I pressed my lips together so I wouldn't laugh. I glanced at Brit to see how she took it. She wouldn't look at me. Apparently she was very interested in her napkin.

Meemaw was notorious for her colorful language.

Ma sent Meemaw a scowl to remind her to watch it. At that moment there was a knock at the door. It was Lars with an overnight bag for Brit.

"Lars, come on in and have some stew," Ma called from the table. "I made a big pot. I used Mary's veggie meat but it turned out good anyway."

"Oh, no thanks, Mrs. Day," Lars said automatically.

"Come have some stew or Jane will fuss," Meemaw said sternly.

"Well, I can't stay . . . " Lars hesitated. "I'm meeting the guys . . . "

"You can eat and run," Meemaw said with finality. She rose and got him a bowl.

Lars seemed reluctant, but once he sat down, he dug in and ate like he was starving.

Ma looked pleased. She liked cooking for people who liked to eat. Albert and I were sort of a disappointment in that way. Albert's tastes were limited; he liked toast, beans and rice, cottage cheese, and bananas. I had gotten pickier, too, because I wasn't into eating meat anymore. I wasn't like, oh, let me lecture you about eating meat because I'm so great. It was just that one day I was at the fair in Sultanville, and I was looking at this cow. She gazed into my eyes and I'm pretty sure she smiled—and that was that. Ma was still adjusting.

"Mary, what did Mr. Shinn say to you?" Ma asked, getting back to the subject.

"He just snuck up behind us acting all mad, and he said we shouldn't be messing around in the woods. And then Brit told him it wasn't his property, but he said we were looking for trouble. He said something else, too—what else did he say, Brit?"

"He said something might *get us*," she answered.

Ma's face turned part angry and part worried. "Something might *get* you? That sounds like a threat."

"I know. It sort of scared me," Brit admitted.

"Plus, it looked like he was carrying a gun," I added.

"Brit, you stay away from there," Lars said. His voice was low and serious.

"I agree with Lars," Ma said. "It sounds like that man's got a screw loose."

"Jane, maybe you should give Bob a call," Meemaw suggested. "It'd start a paper trail, you know?"

Bob Dietz was the sheriff of Adeline.

Ma looked thoughtful. "It's not a bad idea."

I hadn't paid attention to the fact that Albert had been doing a sleepy head-bob for the last few minutes. All of a sudden Albert's head was in his bowl—then he bounced back up with a shocked expression and very messy face. He sent me a groggy memo with a sleepy puppy in it. Sometimes I

37

forgot that even though Albert was crazy-intelligent, he was, after all, just a little boy.

"Oh, Albie, you're tired," I said, laughing.

"Come on, Albert, let's get you cleaned up," Ma said. "You had a big day."

Albert allowed himself to be led away from the table.

Lars stood up. He looked red-cheeked and lanky and very inappropriately dressed for the cold weather in his worn jean jacket and sneakers. "Thanks for dinner, Mrs. Day. It was really good. Later, Albert."

I liked how Lars was so friendly with Albert, even though Albert didn't talk.

"Brit, text me tomorrow if you want a ride," Lars said, buttoning his jacket.

"Mary, why don't you ask Brit if she wants to stay tomorrow night, too," Ma called from the kitchen. She was wiping Albert's face with a washcloth. "It's New Year's Eve. You two can watch the ball drop. Meemaw and I can get some pop and snacks tomorrow."

"You wanna stay over tomorrow?" I asked.

"That'd be nice," Brit said. She looked happy about the invite.

"I'll see you later." Lars carefully shut the door behind him.

Brit had followed Lars to the door. She was looking out the window, her nose pressed against the glass. She waved goodbye to her brother. "It's still snowing," she said softly.

38

8
Sleepover

Everyone else had gone to bed so Brit and I laid out our sleeping bags in the front room. It was more fun sleeping out here than in my bedroom, plus it was cozy by the woodstove. The flames made amber flickers in the little window of the iron door—which sent golden shapes dancing on the ceiling. We had a bowl of popcorn that Meemaw made for us, and we'd eaten most of it.

"You want to check the laptop?" I asked.

"No!" Brit was adamant. "We said we weren't going to look for all of winter break. Remember *the fun-relativity factor*."

"Yeah, I know, you're right. I *have* felt better," I admitted. Brit and I had made this pact to not look at any posts for all of winter break. It made our lame fun seem funner when we weren't comparing our goofy activities to all the spectacular stuff that other kids seemed to be doing. Brit called this *the fun-relativity factor*.

We settled for painting our toenails in ten different

colors, and our fingernails, too. After that, we tried on some false eyelashes that Ma had given me. They made Brit look like a supermodel—after she'd minimized her acne with lots of foundation. But the lashes made me look like Dora the Explorer. I told Brit my comparison, and we both cracked up.

I had to admit that I'd had the same bangs since fifth grade, and I *was* sort of chubby and—well, some might say childish-looking. I used to worry that I wasn't very pretty, but Albert kept sending me messages that contradicted these thoughts. He sent tons of memos with exclamation marks and images of Pearl as a princess—as a great lady in a painting— as an angel with wings—as a sparkling fairy . . . and I began to believe him. I quit thinking about whether I was pretty or not and I just took it for granted that I was awesome, which was a way better way to feel. Pretty nice of Albie.

Brit had laid out Darcy the one-eyed bear next to her pillow. Next to my pillow was Lambert, the limp and graying lamb. His tail was stiff and black because I'd dipped it in paint when I was five. I'd had this vague idea that I was disguising Lambert so Albert wouldn't figure out that the toy was really his. This made zero sense but I wasn't a very smart five-year-old. And of course Albert knew all about my great lamb heist since he was in my brain half of the time. But he didn't comment on things that he didn't care about, and apparently he didn't care about Lambert.

The evening passed without a single memo from my brother. He'd fallen fast asleep after dinner, poor little guy. Ma went ahead and called Sheriff Dietz from her bedroom. We didn't get to hear the conversation, but I felt satisfied that a complaint had been lodged, just in case.

I lay there with my arms behind my head, watching the shadow play of the fire. "You awake, Brit?"

"Yeah, I'm awake."

"Me too," I said.

"*Duh*," she said dryly.

I smiled. "*Duh*."

Brit sighed. "This is nice. I'm glad I'm here. If I were home, I'd have to deal with my mom, or else she'd have Gary over."

"Is he the one with the skeezy mustache?"

"No, that was Roland." Brit grimaced. "He was awful. Gary isn't *as* disgusting, and he distracts her from yelling at me."

"Before my dad died, he was acting all bad-tempered like that."

"What do you think got into him?"

"I don't know. It was like he was having mental problems or something. He was doing his research, and at first he was super happy about it. Ma and I used to visit him out in the garage where he had this really cool lab set up. It was fun to

41

see him out there; he'd let me push buttons and I'd pretend I was a scientist, and Ma helped him a lot with his paperwork. He seemed really psyched about the baby coming, and me starting kindergarten—and then all of a sudden he turned into a jerk."

"Maybe he was drinking or, like, doing drugs," Brit suggested.

"Ma said he didn't do any of that stuff because it was so important for him to think clearly—but maybe he changed. I found a note from him when I was a kid. It was crumpled up in the wastebasket in Ma's room. I didn't even know what it said, but I saved it because I knew it was *his* writing. When I finally learned to read . . . well, it was sort of odd."

"What'd it say?" Brit asked.

"I'll get it. It's in my old diary." I scrambled from the living room to my bedroom and found the little book with the lock and key. I removed the yellowed note that I'd read so many times and brought it out to show Brit.

"It was after the funeral. Ma was really a mess. I think she must have wadded it up and tossed it. Here, you can read it."

Forgive me, my dearest Jane. You are quite right. I'm not myself. I've been cruel to you and Mary, and God help me, I am so sorry. I think I'm losing it. I can't seem to handle

the workload and I can't seem to be a good
father anymore. I feel like I'm cracking up.
Remember that I love you and Mary and the
baby with all my heart and soul. Please, please
remember my love.
                    Forever,
                    Your Albie

Brit solemnly returned the note. "It sounds like he knew he was having problems."

"Yeah, finally he just took off. He was gone for what seemed like a month—but maybe it was less, I can't remember. And then one day the police told Ma there'd been an accident and he was dead. Sometimes I think he meant to drive into that bulkhead."

Brit thought about it for a while. "I know it sounds horrible, but maybe it was good that he left when he did. Maybe he just would have gotten meaner and meaner. At least my mom passes out and then she feels guilty the next day." Brit gave me a grim smile.

"I just wish my dad had gotten help, you know? I could forgive him for being messed up, only he said a lot of bad stuff to Ma, and I'm not sure she'll ever forgive him—especially for leaving us, if that makes any sense. But it's a bummer for her because it takes a lot of energy to stay mad."

"Oh, I know." Brit gave me an expression that said she knew all about that kind of anger. There was a long pause, and she sighed again. "I like your mom."

I giggled. "What about *Meemaw*?"

"Meemaw's tough—I like her, too."

"Yeah, she's okay." The fire snapped and crackled. I felt wide awake. "Hey, do you want to go out and make snow angels?"

"What if the psycho crow is out there?"

"We'll stay close to the house. I'll get the big umbrella."

Brit considered this. "Yeah, okay."

9
Unsettling

We dressed hurriedly, putting our snow clothes on over our pajamas. I grabbed a flashlight and the black umbrella. Before opening the front door, I turned on the porch light and then we tiptoed outside, trying to be quiet. I put the umbrella up for a just-in-case shield, and surveyed the yard and the sky. I could see a whisper of flakes drifting through the halo of light created by the Wagners' oversized halogen. Ken Wagner had nailed the giant light right onto a tree because it was cheaper than erecting a post. Real environmental, Ken.

"Wow, the snow's over my knees." I looked around. "No sign of the crow." I set the umbrella down.

Brit scanned the area, too. "And no freaky animals looking for pancakes." She must have been satisfied with the safety of the yard because suddenly she swooned, falling backward into the snow.

I followed her example and fell back, too. The snow was a cold feather bed. I waved my arms above my head to craft wings, and flapped my legs to make a gown. Delicate snowflakes dappled my face and melted away. Soon we'd made a crowd of angels and we stepped back to admire them. That's when I realized I was hearing the muffled sound of an engine.

"Do you hear a car?" I asked.

"Yes, and it smells familiar." Brit gave me a knowing look.

We peeked around the hedge, and sure enough, there was Lars's pickup in a haze of exhaust.

"Let's see what he's up to," Brit said.

Brit carried the umbrella and I grabbed the flashlight. We slogged to the car where a bass was pounding—but it was just big Tim Guthrie, dozing on the passenger side with his tunes cranked up.

Brit tapped on the window. "Where's Lars?"

Tim spasmed awake. He turned down the sound and lowered his window, allowing a certain smell to waft out. "You scared the farts out of me!" Tim accused.

"Gross," Brit said. "Where's Lars?"

"He wanted to check something out."

Brit frowned. "Check what out?"

"That Shinn guy."

"How long has he been out there?" I asked.

"Too long. If you see him, tell him to get his butt back here. His heater is crap."

"Why don't you go tell him yourself?" Brit countered.

"It's cold out," Tim said, sounding very whiny for such a big guy.

Brit shook her head, disgusted. "Tim, you better make sure your tailpipe is out of the snow or you could asphyxiate yourself from carbon monoxide." She stood there, scowling as he rolled up the window. Under her breath she said, "Tim is such a weenie." She turned to me and her mouth was a tight, worried line. "Mary, I'm nervous about Lars being in those woods. We told him about Mr. Shinn, but we never mentioned that odd mist or how strange the animals were acting."

"I know." I gulped and summoned my courage. "We should go check on him."

"Scoot in and get under the umbrella." Brit linked arms with me and we started walking.

"Is that true—about the tailpipe?" I asked.

"Yeah, it's true. And now he'll have to get out and go check it." She gave me a conspiratorial smile.

We trudged past the garage and onto the trail, losing the light from the back porch. Since the laundry room was also Meemaw's bedroom, she locked the back door and left the light on each night. That door was one of the few things she was nervous about.

I turned the flashlight on. The footprints we'd been following veered to the electric fence and commenced on the other side of the wire. "I don't want to try to jump it," Brit said. "Let's just walk on your side and maybe we'll see him in the field."

When we entered the forest the silence felt heavy; I could hear my heart beating and my breathing was noisy in my ears. There was something unsettling in the air; something that made me feel afraid.

"Lars?" Brit called, but not very loudly.

No answer.

"Hey Brit, there's that red mist." I pointed the flashlight at it.

The little reddish cloud hovered about five feet above the forest floor, maybe fifteen feet from our trail. It was oddly centered in the middle of those six old posts.

"I think it's brighter," Brit observed. She packed a snowball and threw it. It missed and hit one of the posts—which didn't sound like what you would expect from a rotten old post. It rang, like metal.

Brit adjusted her aim and threw another snowball, still trying to hit the mist, and she got it, dead center. The snowball seemed to vanish.

"It's like the fog ate it." I stared into the target. "Throw another one and I'll keep the flashlight right on it." I was aiming the beam of light—when a voice behind me said, "*I told you to stay away from this place.*"

I jumped and squealed—and was hugely relieved to see that it was only Lars.

"Lars, you scared us!" Brit cried, smacking her brother's arm.

"I didn't like what you said about Shinn carrying a gun around," Lars said. "So I thought I'd check things out."

"You see anything?" Brit asked.

"Naw." He grinned a little. "It was a dumb idea and my feet are like ice cubes."

"Tim wants you to hurry back. He said your heater sucks," I related.

"Tim is a weenie. What are *you* two doing out here?" His expression had turned severe.

"I had to be sure you were okay." Brit leaned in and shoved her brother's arm with her shoulder. "Plus, look over there, Lars." She pointed at the ball of mist. "Do you see something glowing?"

"Yeah, I see it; a little cloud, like the size of a basketball." Lars moved his head from side to side. "It's kind of a reddish color. It's more visible if you don't look right at it. I wonder if it's a reflection from an arcing wire or something."

"Throw another snowball at it, Brit," I suggested. I held the flashlight beam steady, illuminating the cloud.

Brit aimed and threw again. The snowball disappeared like the first one, and the impact seemed to make the cloud wobble—or was it the air around the cloud?

"That's really weird," Lars said under his breath. "I have a bad feeling about this. I want you girls to come on." He gave Brit a nudge and they started walking. I still had a snowball in my hand, so I tossed it and actually hit the target. The air did a definite wobble, and I started to feel sick, like the way I felt when the Wagners' dog, Walter, got run over by the garbage truck. It was a feeling of utter dread—and horror, like the forest was haunted by evil spirits that wanted nothing more than to get into my head. My mind became a fever of icky red thoughts. I wanted to call out but my throat got stuck.

I was shocked to realize that Albert was standing next to me, but when I looked in his face his dark eyes seemed to be sneering at me. This idea popped into my head—that Albert was plotting against me. The notion burned in my brain, filling me with hatred. How dare he sneak into my mind whenever he wanted? Just because he thought he was so special and brilliant—

Pearl! Albert's memo seemed to slap me, interrupting my dark train of thought. He filled my brain with a cold, empty memo. The cold cleanliness of it squeezed out the red fever and froze the bad thoughts. In the middle of this cool, clean memo there was a tiny red thought, and the thought said *RUN!*

10
Ball of evil

I scrambled to catch up with Brit and Lars. "Get away from here!" I cried. "This place is bad."

They caught my panic and we all took off running. Brit tossed the umbrella and I dropped the flashlight. I stumbled through the snow as best I could, dragging Albert along with me. But he kept the clean memo in my mind—except for a fraction of a second when I envisioned an image of red spiders covering us and scuttling into our ears.

Albert's hand was still in mine when we reached the side yard. The light from the porch showed that poor Albert was in his jammies and snow boots—actually, he only had one boot on. The other one was gone. I'd been dragging him along with one bare foot!

"Oh, Albie, you've lost your boot. Come here." I picked him up to get his cold tootsies out of the snow and struggled to carry him back to the house.

"Give him to me," said Lars.

I handed Albert to Lars, and Albert didn't object.

"Albert, what was that?" I asked as we tromped along.

His memo was brief: **Bad order**.

I translated for Brit and Lars. "Albert said it was bad order back there."

"But what does that mean?" Brit asked.

"What do you mean by bad order?" I demanded.

Albert memoed **No worries for Pearl.**

"Yeah, it's too late, Albie. I'm worried. Come on, you must have a theory. Does the red mist have anything to do with how those animals were acting?"

All relate. More information is needed. Albert included a padlock that clicked in his memo, which meant he wasn't going to talk about it anymore. I knew it was fruitless to keep pestering him.

I puffed out my frustration. "Albert says he doesn't want to worry us—which means there's definitely something to worry about. But he won't tell me until he figures it out. Did you guys get some bad feeling back there?"

"I absolutely got bad feelings," Lars said. "I'm embarrassed to say it, but I was really pissed off at you two. I mean I was, like, seething."

"So was I!" Brit chimed in. "For a minute I was hating you guys, which doesn't make any sense because I feel the opposite of that. It was almost like that mist was causing hallucinations, or else it was a ball of evil."

When we reached the porch, Lars set Albert down on the mat. "Brit, I'm serious, don't you go back there again," Lars ordered.

"I have no intention of going back!"

"Do you think we should call the police?" I asked.

"And say *what*?" Lars shook his head. "If Sheriff Dietz goes snooping around, I think that stuff could hurt him. I don't know how, but that mist is dangerous."

Albert got tired of waiting and went inside.

"Mary, you should go in and get Albert warmed up," Lars said. "We'll talk about this tomorrow." Lars shoved his hands in his pockets and turned away. Brit and I watched him slog through the snow to his truck.

It was after eleven when I checked the clock in the kitchen. I made some tea to warm us up, and Brit and I took it into the front room to sip by the fire.

I'd put Albert to bed with a hot water bottle on his feet, but as I blew on my tea I got a distracted memo from him: **Police to Danger**, with a split-second glimpse of red spiders—I wasn't sure if he meant to show me that.

"Albert thinks we should *not* call the police," I said to Brit.

She nodded, accepting it. Brit was used to me translating Albert's memos and she believed me 100 percent. But come to think of it, it was surprising that Lars hadn't questioned the silent messaging back on the trail. Unless . . .

"Hey Brit, did you tell Lars about Albert's memos?"

"Yeah, I told him . . . a long time ago," she said with no apology. "Mary, Lars is like me—he knows how to keep a secret."

The second she said this I knew she was right. Brit and Lars were a trustworthy team. If anyone knew how to keep quiet, they did. The only reason I worried about this was that Albert had memoed me when he was a toddler to be discreet about his talent—*discreet* was his word, not mine. I guess he had a good reason for his secrecy but he hadn't made that clear—not yet, anyhow.

"I trust you guys," I said. I leaned against Brit and gave her a nudge.

The fire in the woodstove cracked, and I jumped. I was still on edge.

"What do you think is out there?" Brit asked.

I thought of the horror and the hatred that had paralyzed me and the image of red spiders filling up my ears. I sort of doubted the reality of those spiders. I had a feeling that Albert was trying to put something complicated into a shape I could understand. But even if there were no red spiders in the woods . . . it was something bad.

"I have no idea what that stuff is," I said, "but Albert is trying to figure it out."

"Do you think we should wake up your mom?"

"I don't know. No, let her sleep. I guess we'll tell her in the morning."

11
THE TRIAD CONFIRMS A GROSS IMBALANCE

The data was accurate and it did not bode well for this sector. The Commodore and his counterparts scanned it again, and they concurred. The triad directed the data with a concentrated code into the entangled hub (which Citizen Lady liked to call *the can*). The response was almost immediate: ALL SMHR UNITS RETURN.

The triad conferred for many more seconds before they all agreed: The Commodore, Med Tech Tek, and Citizen Lady would suggest that this triad of smart-mass-holograph-research units would stay in the sector, regardless of the danger it posed. Of course SMHR units would not be affected by the unwelcome leakage as they were not biological beings and, thus, did not possess a vulnerable consciousness. For them, the real danger lay in the gross imbalance. If the leak continued and worsened, the equations predicted a dimensional exchange. Now that was risky. But it was also fascinating. The triad declared that this was an invaluable opportunity to collect data. It wasn't every day that a dimensional universe faced annihilation.

The home-plane agreed that this was so, but only one SMHR unit would stay because they were far too valuable to squander in a disaster, as was their SMHR craft, which was integral.

Once again the triad conferred, and once again they agreed: they would stay put, all three of them, along with their integral craft. They were accustomed to each other, and their individual sequences were complementary to the whole. Besides, they were not inclined to return to the home-plane in the midst of such interesting events.

112000x, 113000x, and 114000x feigned a system malfunction; thus, the regretful action of noncompliance. This report caused the home-plane to immediately spew equations opposing this thin claim. If the SMHR units had been in their solid-mass forms, they would have showed their teeth and made laughter, imitating the odd vocalization of human amusement—this mimicry never failed to tickle their sequences.

Luckily, Med Tech Tek had written programs, oh, some twenty Earth-years before that would deny auto-access by the home-plane. The triad was pleased with Med Tech Tek's foresight, because now they could do whatever they wanted.

Yet unexpectedly, the Commodore, Med Tech Tek, and Citizen Lady became aware of an edginess in their synapses—an uncomfortable sharpness at the base of their emotional algorithm. They endured it for three long seconds until Citizen Lady identified the conflict.

"Anxiety," she said. "We are experiencing *worry*."

"Worry? Worry about what?" the Commodore sputtered.

"About this place, these beings," Citizen Lady said.

"We have learned much from the Extraordinary Mind *and* his sister," Med Tech Tek agreed. "Being stationed here has been both revealing and invigorating."

The Commodore would have nodded his head if he had been in his solid mass form—he'd grown so accustomed to using that affirmative gesture. "How might we stop this uncomfortable synapse?" he inquired. "This *anxiety* is most vexing."

Once again, Citizen Lady had the answer. "Interfere," she said. "Ignore protocol and try to help."

The Commodore felt—yes, he *felt*—a sense of exhilaration. Indeed, this was the answer. The mere consideration of *helping* dispelled the distracting anxiety. He shared this reaction with his counterparts and the triad was unified in buoyant agreement. Oh, they would collect data, to be sure, but he and Med Tech Tek and Citizen Lady were all quite resolute in a logic sequence that seemed very clear; this triad could be useful in the coming crisis. *This* smart-mass–holograph-research triad meant to be of service.

12
Bad neighborhood

All night I dreamed of that thing in the woods. Over and over again I was being chased by flying red spiders that were trying to get into my ears. At the last possible minute I'd get a snowy, cold memo from Albert that would deter them, but then I'd forget about the protective image and the spiders would start in again. It was exhausting. I was glad to wake up.

I realized I was in the living room in a sleeping bag, and the morning light was hopeful and bright. I thought about the scary encounter the night before and the nightmares that ruined my sleep. It made me think how real those bad feelings were—how they created an awful reality and an awful me. Maybe *good* feelings could be just as real. Maybe good thoughts made their own reality, too. This idea made me feel a lot better.

I shuffled to the kitchen and discovered we'd slept in. There was a note on the fridge from Ma. I squinted to focus my eyes:

Hi, kids. They plowed Myrtle Road, so I'm going to try to get Meemaw to her foot-care appointment at the Senior Center. If skies stay clear, we'll have lunch there and will get groceries at Top Shelf. We'll pick up some goodies for tonight. You girls can make snacks and can toast the New Year with sparkling cider! Eat a good breakfast. See that Albert gets dressed and eats something, too.

Love, Ma and Meemaw

Brit and I sat at the dining room table, all groggy and dull. In front of us were sloppy bowls of cereal. We ate just to eat. I felt dreary from my rotten sleep, and Brit looked like a zombie.

Today's newspaper was on the table. It had a headline about New Year's Eve.

Brit turned to look at the paper. "*Bleh*. I hate New Year's."

"I know," I agreed. "And what's the big deal about dropping a ball? Big *whup*, another year." I knew she hated it because of her mom, but we didn't need to talk about that.

"Yeah, big *whup*," she said in a small voice.

"Hey, Albert, come eat your breakfast!" I yelled.

I'd made him toast and peeled a banana that had some bruises. It didn't look very appetizing.

Surprisingly, Albert came to the table fully dressed in his

60

jeans and a pullover. He'd kept his *Star Wars* jammy-shirt on underneath, but still . . . this was pretty thorough for Albert. He even had his shoes on—though it was the single boot from last night and a sneaker. "Good job getting dressed, Albert." I gave him a thumbs-up.

Brit was reading a sci-fi paperback. Lars must have tossed it in the bag with Darcy, which was nice of him. He acted tough a lot of the time, but I imagined that it was just habit— like for protection, living where he lived and all. There'd been lots of sketchy boyfriends that their mom had brought home. Brit told me that Lars had punched one of the guys in the face and told him to get the hell out and never come back. And that was when he was only fourteen. Yeah, Lars was okay.

I studied Brit for a second. Her hair was frizzed-out on the side that she'd slept on, and her skin was pale beneath her acne. Her eyes looked very blue, like sparkling jewels that matched the sky-blue sweater she wore.

"That color looks good on you, Brit. It makes your eyes look really pretty." I'd given her the sweater because I didn't like it anymore. It was a turtleneck—I didn't like stuff around my neck.

She glanced up. "Thanks." Her cheeks went pink and she didn't look like such a zombie. Then she stuck her nose back in her book.

Albert nibbled his toast.

I ate another spoonful of cereal.

A cold, bright sun was shining into the dining room. It showed how dirty our windows were and it illuminated a billion dust particles. This would please Albert. He'd always enjoyed studying floating particulate—*particulate* was his word, not mine. He liked to clump particles into organized designs, like those puzzles where you find the patterns, only Albert's dust game was so complicated that I didn't get it *at all*.

None of us mentioned the night before. Brit yawned. Albert stared at the dust. My eyes brushed the newspaper again—and I noticed this horrible headline. It said, "Adeline man mauled by his own dog."

"*Whoa*! Brit, listen to this: 'Long-time resident of Adeline, Ralph J. Hinkey, was mauled by his seven-year-old Labrador, Beau. Beau had never exhibited violent behavior and was well loved by the family. The dog was put down and an autopsy is being performed to verify physiological abnormalities such as brain injury or rabies. Hinkey was declared dead at Providence Hospital.'"

"We know Beau!" Brit cried.

"They live on the other side of the power line," I said soberly. "Beau was a nice dog. And Mr. Hinkey is dead. Oh my God, Brit."

"Mary, could it be related to the thing in the woods?"

I turned to look at Albert. Mr. Hinkey and Beau used to walk the power line all the time. Albert must have been considering what Brit and I suspected—that the red mist was involved in this somehow, but he refused to send me a memo that might explain the awful event. He just continued to look at the dust.

"Does Albert know what happened?" Brit asked.

"He's not telling me a thing, but—" The landline rang and I jumped up to answer it.

"Hello?"

"If it's your mom, tell her maybe she should come home," Brit said with an anxious face.

I shook my head. "It's not her," I whispered. "It's my uncle."

"We're fine—No, she isn't home right now; she and Meemaw went to town—Yes, I just saw something about that, but honestly, that is just bizarre—No, we've never had a break in—No, Albert doesn't run around by himself!—Our neighbors are mostly nice—Really, my school is okay—I miss Andy, too—I'll tell my mom you called—Goodbye."

I hung up the phone with a frown on my face. "That was my uncle Joe, my dad's brother over in Appledale."

"What was he saying about your secret twin?" Brit was smirking and pointing her eyes at the picture of my cousin above the buffet. With Andy's chopped bangs and wide face, he looked like the boy version of me.

I smirked back. "Uncle Joe said that Andy missed me,

which I sorta doubt. Anyway, he saw the news about Beau on TV. He was basically telling me that we live in a crappy neighborhood and we should move to Appledale where I could go to Saint Theresa's with Andy and live happily ever after."

"You do live in a crappy neighborhood," Brit conceded, "and I bet Saint Theresa's is fantastic, but unfortunately, I only have one best friend."

"Same," I agreed with a wry smile.

My Uncle Joe and Aunt Rita had been after Ma for a long time, trying to get her to move to Appledale, which actually sounded kind of fun to me. But I couldn't leave Brit, and Ma seemed to be stuck in one gear—like she could handle her life if absolutely nothing else changed.

There was a knock at the door, and Lars poked his head in.

"Lars!" Brit said.

"I thought I'd check on you guys." He shut the door behind him and came into the dining room. His sneakers left snow-tread on the floor.

"You want some cereal?" I asked. "I know how to make coffee if you like coffee."

"Naw, I'm good."

"Did you see this, Lars?" Brit handed him the article about Mr. Hinkey.

"No." His lips were pressed together in a little frown. "If I *had* seen it, I don't think I would have walked back there just now."

"And you told me not to go!" Brit scolded.

"Was it still there?" I asked.

"It was faint but it was there. And it was bigger. I stayed away from it."

We were all surprised by *another* rap at the door.

"Lars, did you call the police?" I asked.

He shook his head.

I got up to answer but first I peeked out the front-room window. "Brit!" I hissed. "Come check out these guys."

She rushed over to sneak a peek by the sill. "They look like those door-to-door church people," Brit said.

"I've seen them before . . . " A dreamy feeling came over me, and my cereal got squishy in my stomach. "When I was a little kid, I—Brit, I don't think they're church guys. Let's pretend we're not home."

While Brit and I were trying to slink back to the dining room, Albert went and opened the front door.

It was them! It was the same weirdos who'd given me the pamphlet when Albie was just a baby.

13
The visitors . . . *again*

I couldn't believe it. I'd always sort of thought it was a dream because my memory of the event seemed so . . . warped. But it was them, all right.

Albert hurried away down the hall, and then he returned. In his hand was a framed picture of a sweet little puppy on a swing. He turned it over and behind the wire was *the pamphlet*. Years ago he had memoed me to hide it. In fact, he had still been a baby and couldn't even crawl yet. I'd stuck it behind that picture and put it back on the wall, and I'd forgotten about it all this time.

Albert held the pamphlet out, and the small man took it.

"Thank you," he responded. Then he turned to me and said, "I am the Commodore. We met when you were shorter and less intelligent."

He showed me a smile, and it was just as creepy as I recalled—like piano keys lined up in a row. His small, pale head was completely bald, with ears like little shells. He wore brown-tinted glasses that had fabric on the sides, like the old-timey shades that mountaineers wore to prevent snow blindness. I couldn't see his eyes at all. All three of them wore the same brown-tinted glasses.

The Commodore nudged the tall woman.

"I am Citizen Lady," she said, as if on cue. "A female."

"Your name is *Citizen Lady*?" I asked.

"Yes, that is correct. I am Citizen Lady. A female."

The Commodore shook his head ever so slightly, as if he was trying to get her to shut up.

Citizen Lady commenced smiling the same toothy grin that the Commodore had showed. She was almost as tall as I recalled, and her blunt-cut, yellow hair had an overly shiny look that reminded me of a cheap Halloween wig. She wore the same style black suit as the Commodore and the other guy.

I turned to Brit with my eyes wide and my eyebrows up.

The third guy had dark skin that looked strange in the snowy light. It was too smooth. And his hair looked like it had been painted on his head. He introduced himself. "I am Med Tech Tek of this most effective triad. So pleased to greet you!" He didn't offer a hand to shake, but he smiled and nodded, clicking his teeth softly. All three of them began smiling and doing a bobblehead nod, their teeth clicking away.

"So . . . what do you want?" I asked. I wished they'd quit their grinning and clicking—it was super creepy.

The Commodore ceased his head-bobbing. "We have data to share."

"Hmm. Okay. Thank you!" I started closing the door. All of a sudden, Albert put his little booted foot in the way.

"Albert," I bent over to hiss in his ear, "these guys could be serial killers. Don't encourage them."

Albert promptly sent me a memo that said **Three safe, more info.**

"Albie, you gotta give me more than that."

Three safe—good order, he sent. The words were leafy-green and a butterfly shape floated peacefully through the calm. His memo was insistent—it pulsed green several times.

The strange visitors stood patiently on the porch, lined up tall to short. I looked back at Lars—*he* could be tough. "Lars, what do you think? Should we talk to them?"

Lars came to the door. "I want to see some ID," he said, in a voice as deep and firm as he could muster.

The three weirdos glanced at each other, as if unsure.

"*ID—ID—Identification*," the Commodore proclaimed in a voice that was slightly . . . mechanical. At the same moment, all three reached into their black jacket pockets and pulled out green-tinted cards. The cards were translucent with a bronze shield that had a butterfly center, surrounded by zeros and ones. Albert was standing next to me. He eyed the cards and sent me a memo. **Legitimate**.

"What do you mean, *legitimate*? These cards don't *say* anything!"

Legit, legit, Albert repeated, with the happy butterfly multiplying itself.

I sighed and addressed the visitors. "Okay, what do you want?" I was intentionally trying to sound sharp and tough.

"We'd like to confer about the . . . situation."

"Situation?"

"The anomaly in this area."

"You mean the *mist*?"

"No." Click-click went his teeth. "You are mistaken in naming it *mist*."

"Well, then *what*?"

"A rip," he said. His toothy smile had turned into a frown. "An interdimensional tear. It's allowing unnatural energy into your world and if the imbalance continues, the results will be disastrous."

"Disastrous," they all repeated in unison.

I cast my mind back to the feelings that I'd had in the woods. There was no doubt that the situation was serious, but where did these guys come from? And why did they look and act so weird? I glared at the Commodore. "Are you with the police or, like, a government agency or something?"

This idea came to me when I noticed their shoes. I recalled Meemaw saying that "government men" always wore black shoes, and these three characters did indeed wear black dress shoes with laces that tied—even Citizen Lady, who was, as she'd kept insisting, a *female*.

"Yes, the government," the Commodore said, nodding. The other two bobbed their heads in agreement. Once again they eagerly showed me their cards.

I rolled my eyes. "These don't mean anything to me; they could be Pokémon cards for all I know. But my brother seems to take them seriously."

"Albert knows," the Commodore asserted. He turned to my brother and made a quick, respectful little bow.

"The automobile is ready for departure," Citizen Lady said, like she was hinting that they ought to hurry up.

"We invite you on a fact-finding mission," the Commodore said, gesturing toward the street.

"No way!" I answered with the finality of a guillotine chop. "This is ridiculous. Do you expect us to go somewhere with you? I mean, you guys are totally suspicious showing up with your sunglasses and your sketchy IDs." I was trying to sound rude on purpose. I thought it would make me seem more imposing.

The three characters looked at each other, and then at me.

"Duly noted," the Commodore replied.

"I should have cleaned up the schematic," Med Tech Tek said, displaying his remorse like a sad-faced clown.

The Commodore paid him no mind. "We would not presume on your peaceful lives if the situation did not require it," he said. "Your brother will vouch."

Albert sent me a memo that said **Vouched,** with a sure and certain edge to it.

Normally I trusted Albert 100 percent, but he was in *my* care and I didn't trust these weirdos with their phony cards and silly names.

Albert attached a new memo. **I must go for more information, for good order.** A follow-up memo said **With Pearl—or without.** The memo was unyielding and it sat heavy on my heart. Albert began putting his jacket on. There was no stopping him when he was obsessed like this.

"So tell me the truth, Albert," I said with just a hint of frustration. "Are you admitting that we have something to worry about?"

He responded immediately with a memo that quivered with anxiety. **Yes, the time to worry is <u>now.</u>**

14
To the—er—*lab*

"**O**kay Albert, we'll go. But I swear if you're wrong about these guys, I'm going to be so mad at you!" I ran and got my coat. I was still in P.J. bottoms and a T-shirt and had my kitty-cat slippers on my feet. I kicked off the slippers and found my boots.

"Mary, you can't go without *me*." Brit sounded offended. "What would I say to your mom? And your Meemaw would kill me."

"You rug-gnats can't go by yourselves." Lars turned to the people on the porch. "You've got to leave one of those cards—*and* your driver's license."

The Commodore immediately handed over his translucent green card with the ones and the zeros and the butterfly shield. Then he turned to Med Tech Tek, who abruptly raised his hand and showed a driver's license that he had hidden in his palm.

"We are from another town," Med Tech Tek said. "We are from . . . *New York*."—They all said *New York* at the same time. Once again, Brit and I exchanged a wary glance.

I looked at the driver's license—#MEDTECH 112000x—with some crazy New York address that was, like, *101010 Smhru Street*.

Lars took both pieces of ID and set them on the dining room table. "I guess if we don't come back, the cops will know where to start looking." Lars gave Med Tech Tek a stern expression, showing him that we weren't just dumb kids.

Med Tech Tek smiled back, bobbing his head in agreement. "Indeed," he said. "The identification will be most revealing."

His comment made me nervous. Would a serial killer say something like that?

Brit grabbed her jacket and put on her boots, and then we followed the three weirdos across the yard. The bright sun of a few moments ago had been snuffed by a sudden, thick fog. The fog made our yard quiet, like a quiet room with a snowy carpet. It made the street quiet, too. I could hardly see ten feet in front of me and it gave me a dreamlike feeling. I wondered about the last twenty-four hours—the red mist, the crow, and now these strange people with their "fact-finding mission." Pausing midstep I said, "With the snow and the fog, and you three government guys, this feels like a weird dream."

"It is not a dream," the Commodore responded with authority. "This reality is a conscious, real-time event. It has no distortions or other possibilities. It could only happen this way, and in fact, it always happened this way."

"Mr. Commodore, I don't know what you're talking about, but what you said makes everything seem *weirder.*" I gave him a glare.

Albert sent me a comforting memo. **Pearl has good sense**. It had the equivalent of a smiley pearl which was Albert's way of sending his love.

We followed the government guys to where they had parked. There, in the smothering fog of the cul-de-sac, was an old-model Volkswagen Bug with its engine running. It was white outside and white on the inside, too, with bench seats in the front and back.

"How are we supposed to all fit in that thing?" Brit asked.

"Through the doors, which open," said the Commodore. He and Med Tech Tek and Citizen Lady scrunched into the front bench seat; Citizen Lady's yellow hair brushed the ceiling. Me and Brit and Lars and Albert squeezed into the back.

"FYI, there are no seat belts back here," I announced.

The Commodore began to stammer. *"FYI—FYI—F—*

for your information," he said with a hint of triumph in his voice.

"Right." I pursed my lips and raised my eyebrows so Brit would see. She did the same back. "Well, we can't buckle up," I pointed out.

"Seat belts," the Commodore exclaimed, directing this comment toward Med Tech Tek.

"Oops," said Med Tech Tek. He made a chuckling sound that bubbled out in crazy notes and pitches—it made me want to laugh, too. These guys might be super weird, but their laughter put me at ease.

Citizen Lady was in the driver's seat. "Let's go!" she said cheerfully. The car jerked slightly and hummed, but it seemed like the hum was more in my bones than in my ears. Moments passed and except for the dull hum, the car seemed very quiet and still, like an electric car—only this model was too old for that. I looked around. The interior was plush, pale leather, with vintage crank-windows and shiny chrome door locks. The windows were heavily tinted; I peered out but I could hardly see a thing. The dark windows and the thick fog gave me a strange feeling that we were moving *up*. I forced a yawn and my ears popped.

"Citizen Lady, are you sure you can see well enough to drive?" I asked. "It looks like a sea of cotton balls out there."

"I will refer to my instruments," she assured me.

I checked the dashboard but it revealed nothing. "Maybe you should turn on your lights," I suggested.

"Indeed I should, for your health," she agreed.

The interior of the car lit up with a violet-colored light . . . and then I couldn't see anything at *all* outside. I gave up on being a backseat driver.

"Where are we going?" Lars asked.

"To the—er—*lab*," the Commodore said.

"And here we are!" Citizen Lady announced.

"What do mean, 'here we are'? We've been in the car for, like, three minutes. That wouldn't even get us off Myrtle Road." I hated to argue with them but they were so ridiculous.

"The fog is deceptive," the Commodore said. "Time and space can be difficult to measure with sensory criteria."

I tossed Brit another *What the hay?* face.

We found ourselves in a small garage where the walls were finished in the same pale leather as the interior of the car. They curved to meet the floor, and there were some modern details of chrome stripes at the base and ceiling.

"This place is cool," I said. "I can't believe you put leather upholstery in a garage."

"We would never be so uncivilized as to decorate with skin," the Commodore stiffly objected.

"Dear bovines," Citizen Lady added. Her face went sad-clown and her teeth clicked with disapproval.

"This way," Med Tech Tek said. He ushered us through a door that must have been an elevator. Moments later, the door opened and we entered a large, round room—that is, it was shaped like a doughnut with the elevator where the doughnut hole would have been. The outer walls of the room were bare and curved. There were no windows in the smooth white walls, which seemed a little bit creepy.

"So here is the problem," the Commodore said. He directed our attention to the far wall which lit up and became a video screen. On the screen was a picture of my dad! Like it was no big deal, the Commodore said, "Your father, Albert E. Day, caused the rip."

15
The weight of order

The mention of my father startled me; it seemed so out of context. "Wait, what?"

"Albert E. Day was experimenting with thought fractals and he was successful in this procedure," the Commodore explained.

"But what does that mean?" I asked.

"He discovered a delivery system that carries communication via thought patterns. For example, imagine one limb of a tree," the Commodore began. "Picture the tip has three star-like points, and the middle point of *that* has three star-like points, and the middle point of *that* has three star-like points . . . And so it goes, smaller and smaller until the measurement is at the quantum level, and still it gets smaller. The structure of the thought-fractal can be sent in coded streams. This stream can 'dig' a tunnel, similar to what you call a wormhole, and then carry the messages within."

Citizen Lady interrupted. "Albert E. Day utilized this fractal algorithm and found his way into the half-constant."

"What's the half-constant?" I asked.

"Another dimension," Citizen Lady answered. "A dimension that exists here and now, but in its own reality. It's where your thoughts go. The positive and the negative thoughts of your universe swirl and interact in the half-constant until they find their place in the scheme of things. It's a delicate balance. It is good order."

"Obviously the weight of order has been disturbed," said Med Tech Tek with his exaggerated frown.

A movie began to play on the wall screen; it was my dad in his old lab in the garage at home. I was shocked to see him like this. I felt embarrassed and flustered because it was so up-close and intimate. He looked scruffy and boyish, like maybe how Albert would look when he grew up. But the man seemed happy and excited—nothing like the gruff, hostile father that was stuck in my memory.

"You see," the Commodore went on, "there was evidence that an imbalance was occurring. The triad—that is, *we*— detected turbulence and pressure at the quantum level some time ago. But when your father attempted his experiments, his probe opened a valve, so to speak."

On the screen my dad was hooking electrode gizmos onto his head, and these were attached to a machine that was wired to his computer.

"Where did you get this video?" I asked. The shock of seeing my dad seemed to dry out my mouth and twist my stomach in a knot. My privacy felt violated; *our* privacy as a family.

"We copied this from your father's records," Med Tech Tek said. He seemed unaware of my discomfort. "Here, your father is amplifying the impulses from his own mind and sending that information to a trans-coder in his computer. From there the package is sent to the lasers in the woods."

Albert nodded.

Scornfully, I said, "There are no lasers in our woods." But then I remembered the ringing tone of the post when Brit tossed that first snowball.

"They were small, but with the convergence of six of them and with the boost from the power lines, they were effective. The connection was accomplished with the most basic technology. Very admirable for such primitive tools." Med Tech Tek nodded to Albert as he said this.

"But you said my dad *caused* the rip."

"He certainly hurried it along," Med Tech Tek said. "But, to be fair, if the pressure had not been so great, the tear would have naturally sealed. The pressure was great because the imbalance was great; the negative ratio was overwhelming."

"Really, it was fortuitous that your father identified the problem before it followed its natural conclusion," Citizen Lady said kindly.

Now the screen was showing a math sequence that was stupefying. The numbers and symbols began to graph down and down into the shape of a funnel, until it ended in a teeny-tiny ring—and then, *BLAM*, all the numbers squeezed through the ring and exploded inside out. It was a sickening display of chaos.

I closed my eyes and rubbed them. "That's giving me a headache."

Brit moved closer to me and touched my arm. She definitely looked worried now. I didn't understand what the numbers meant, but I think Brit had an inkling of what these equations were all about.

The screen went dark. "As you can plainly see, the *natural conclusion* is alarming," said Med Tech Tek. He made a grim expression, which the other two weirdos imitated. I noticed that they all kept their dark glasses on, so I couldn't see their eyes. It made me doubt their honesty. It made me feel like they were trying to trick me with pictures of my dad that got me emotional and confused.

"The imbalance is what concerns us," Med Tech Tek finally said. "It will affect this reality. Albert understands."

"Yeah, but I don't!" I snapped. I was impatient with Med

Tech Tek and the Commodore and Citizen Lady. I felt like they weren't being truthful.

"Why were you spying on my dad in the first place—and why don't you take those glasses off? It's not even bright in here." Without thinking, I flipped a careless hand at Med Tech Tek, and his dark glasses went flying.

"What the—" Lars reached for Brit and made her back away.

I backed up, too, and tried to fit what I saw into a context that was familiar—which was impossible. Med Tech Tek had no eyes.

16
Stunned

I should have been more thorough," Med Tech Tek said. His smooth skin and fake-looking hair seemed totally monstrous with only the plane of his face where his eyes should have been. He walked directly to where his glasses had fallen and retrieved them with amazing accuracy. His lack of eyeballs didn't seem to affect his ability to detect where things were.

"I take full responsibility," he said, sounding very sorry. "The original schematic was hasty, and I admit that I never bothered to fine-tune it." He put his glasses back on his face and assumed the body language of hunched shoulders and a hanging head that communicated shame.

"I told you back on the porch that this would be problematic," the Commodore snapped.

"Commodore, any of us could have completed that task. We all put it 'on the back burner,' as they say. We can adjust the schematic tonight." Citizen Lady was trying to keep the peace. She turned to face us. "We'll have our eyeballs on tomorrow," she assured us. "We don't want you uncomfortable with . . . inaccuracies."

"Oh, I think it's a little late for that," Brit said. "Who are you people, really?"

Citizen Lady was contrite. "We are not from New York." She shook her head sadly.

"*Duh*," I said under my breath.

"In fact, we are not *people*, as such," she said haltingly. "We are SMHR units."

"*Smerunis*?" Is that your nationality?" asked Brit.

"No. *S-M-H-R unit* stands for 'smart-mass-holograph-research unit,' and it's a designation—a category," Citizen Lady explained.

Brit made an impatient face.

"We are here to gather data. We come from far away," she added.

"Like outer space?" Brit asked.

"Yes, space that is . . . out there." Citizen Lady made a sweeping gesture.

"So, you are researchers, and you came to Earth to study things," I confirmed.

"Exactly," said the Commodore. He seemed relieved.

"And then you saw this problem with the half-thingy leaking," I went on.

"Precisely." His head bobbed enthusiastically. "We detected the problem—and hypothesized that a solution would include your counterpart, Albert."

"Albert?" I repeated.

"Yes. As you know, he has a superlative mind as well as exceptional emotional depth. Observe this copy of one of your father's digital records." The Commodore stood aside and the video screen blinked on again. This time it was a poorly lit view of both my parents in our garage laboratory. The viewpoint didn't change; Dad must have propped a camera on the shelf. My mom was sitting in a chair and my dad was messing with some wires and plugs. She looked much younger and very pretty in jeans and a T-shirt with her sandy hair in a ponytail. Dad was dark and handsome, and it struck me what a beautiful couple they were.

Ma once told me that Meemaw didn't like my dad at first, that Meemaw's head was filled with super negative ideas about anyone who was different from her. My dad was "a city slicker," according to Meemaw. And he was an "egghead college boy who thought he was *all that*." Turned out she couldn't help but like him because he was so calm and humble and sweet to her. She had to change her tune, Ma said. Calm, humble, sweet. I suddenly missed the dad I'd barely had with such longing that it made me want to cry.

On the screen my mom was laughing—the sound was

overly loud, like bad acoustics. "I feel like Frankenstein," she said. "And that stuff is cold!" She shuddered as my dad applied some gel, and then stuck metal circles connected to wires onto her scalp and forehead. "I want to get dinner on, and Mary will be back from the Stickles' any minute."

"I know," young Dad replied. "Okay, I already set up the algorithms, and now I can see if the electronics coordinate. Ready? This will just take a second . . . "

I looked over at Albert. He was nodding his head, like, yep, that's what happened.

My dad flipped a toggle-switch, adjusted a dial, and then reached behind his back and moved a large lever. He flipped it on, and then flipped it off again—my mom blinked her eyes, but that was all.

"Well, they're all synching." Dad was obviously pleased as he examined his screens and machines. "Feel anything, Jane?"

"I don't think so—now get these things off of me. I'm in the middle of making lasagna. *Eww*, now my hair's all sticky!"

"Thanks for the help, hon. Sorry about the slime." He kissed her cheek, and she disappeared out of the video's line of focus. Dad must have turned the recorder off because the screen went black.

Citizen Lady bent down to better face me. In a

sympathetic voice, she said, "Your mother did not know it, but she was pregnant when that test was attempted. There was a brief connection to the half-constant, and young Albert was altered by the link. The triad—that is, *we*—consider him to be our best hope."

Another shock. I was stunned, really. I had never thought about why Albert was the way he was. He was just *Albie*—my smart and funny little guy—who was definitely a bit of an introvert.

"Albert, did it hurt?" I asked him quietly. I wasn't sure if I was mad at my parents or not.

Albert sent a memo that described being startled by hundreds of birds launching into flight, at first noisy and chaotic as they flapped and rose, but then they synchronized, dipping, swirling, rising in a beautiful dance. **It did not hurt**, he assured me in strong, solid letters.

"But did you get any bad feelings?"

His next memo showed me a spider and a butterfly; the spider gnashed his cartoon teeth while the butterfly peacefully fluttered about. But I got the feeling that these creatures were far away from Albert, and whatever their issues were, that stuff didn't touch him. **Safe glimpses**, he added.

I was trying to figure out what a safe glimpse of a spider and a butterfly meant when the Commodore said, "After we detected high-level patterning emanating from your sibling, we began to monitor the Day domicile."

"Spy on us, you mean," I accused him. I scanned the interior of the round "laboratory" and I looked at these eyeless, black-suited people who claimed to be from outer space. I turned to my brother. "Albert, these guys, these SMHR units—are they for real? I mean, are they, like, good and *nice*?"

Good and Nice! Albert's memo blinked with absolute conviction in a brown-and-blue color that seemed final and true.

"I guess Albert believes in you," I said, "even with your no-eyeball thing going on."

"But why are Brit and I here?" Lars asked. He'd been so quiet up to this point, but now he stepped forward and said, "You three seem pretty deliberate about the plans you make and the stuff you do, so why'd you let me and Brit come along?" His face was even paler than usual and his hands were stuffed in his jacket pockets like he was hiding his fists.

"You all play a part," Citizen Lady acknowledged. "Albert is the key, but Pearl is compassionate. Equationaut is clever. And Lars is brave. Excellent counterparts if one were to encounter an emergency."

17
Shivering space and time

Pardon me, but we ought to depart if we are to observe the other dimensional tear. I'll drive," the Commodore said firmly, but then he made one of his chuckling sounds and the other two joined in. Some private joke about driving, I guessed.

I imagined that we would get back in the car that was parked downstairs in the garage, but the Commodore just stood there. They all just stood there. Suddenly the wall came to life, glowing faintly violet. Symbols came and went so fast they looked like pulsing static.

Citizen Lady glanced our way. "For your health, you must stand in the field-shower." She pointed to where Albert was already standing. On the floor, a large violet square lit up. Brit and Lars and I checked each other with anxious expressions and then hurried to stand in the square. I looked up to see an identical square on the ceiling, and between the two, a faint light shimmered—as if we were in a *Star Trek* transporter. It made my gums itch.

"So this isn't just a lab, is it?" Brit said. "It's a spacecraft, right?"

"It is both," said Med Tech Tek.

"And are these squares some kind of electromagnetic shield?"

"A photon shield for your health," Med Tech Tek affirmed.

"Citizen Lady, shouldn't you guys get in your squares, you know, for your health?" I asked.

"We are SMHR units and one with our craft, so of course there is no bother." She smiled to reassure me. "I devised this apparatus for human health," she added, obviously proud of her invention.

I half expected to be transported somewhere, but we just stood there in the violet light. There was a whirring and a pulse on one of the wall screens. Minutes passed and I watched a steady rhythm of yellow to violet ticking away on the screen; it gave me a sleepy feel. There was that low hum I'd felt in the Volkswagen, along with the drowsy buzz of the "field-shower." I tried sticking my finger outside of the shimmering square and I felt a bit of a shock. I decided to keep my hands and feet inside and not mess around.

"The Commodore is an excellent navigator," Citizen

Lady said. She smiled at the small, pale man who appeared to be concentrating on the wall screen. He began to recite some techie lingo in a blank, mechanical tone: "Engage torus drive—space/time shiver enacted—field density accomplished—proceed."

I heard no engine and felt no thrust; I was a little disappointed.

"I would nudge it 0.02 percent in the forward field for maximum efficiency," Med Tech Tek suggested.

The Commodore ignored him; all his attention was on the screen.

"Don't be a backseat driver," Citizen Lady scolded. But then she made a chuckle to show she was teasing Med Tech Tek. Her lilting squawk made me want to laugh, too. I wondered if she borrowed the term from me—*backseat driver*—had I said that out loud in the Volkswagen? I couldn't remember.

"Mr. Commodore, what do you mean by a space/time shiver?" I asked. "It sounds neat."

He didn't answer. He was absolutely frozen, concentrating on the screen.

Med Tech Tek answered instead. "*Shiver* is a colloquial term—Citizen Lady coined it." He smiled and clicked his teeth. "We excite the space/time around our craft with an oscillating pulse. Using this method our craft merely *parks* within a shivering pocket of manipulated space so that it is the *space* that moves us. That's how we cheat the speed limit." He grinned and nodded, amused with his explanation, which I really didn't get.

"It's warp speed," Brit said. "It's like you compress the space in front and expand the space behind really fast—like a pulse—and inside this bubble the craft is floating on a wave of rolling space/time. Something like that."

"Whoa, that's cool," I remarked.

"Indeed, for superconductivity, it must be." Med Tech Tek was done conversing, and he, too, turned his attention to the screen.

Time passed. It seemed like after a while the SMHR units began to look transparent, and so did the walls of the craft. I rubbed my eyes. Yes, I could see stars out there— only they looked watery and they seemed to stretch around our "bubble."

It was hard to figure how much time went by. Albert wasn't sending me memos; I guess his mind was elsewhere. He loved this sort of thing. I was startled when Citizen Lady said, "Here we are!"

At once the SMHRs and their lab became solid. Now the wall screens were showing what appeared to be a giant movie of a planet. The movie made it look like we were moving from dark space to atmosphere and the atmosphere had a reddish hue. On the round planet below, there were no oceans and not much variance in color, and not a hint of civilization.

I started to think that I wasn't watching a movie, but that I was looking out of a window. "There's no ocean down there," I said. "That can't be Earth."

"Correct," said the Commodore. "That is not Earth."

The land got larger. We seemed to be descending but it didn't feel like we were. I knew that in an elevator or on a ride at the carnival, my stomach would be lurching upward.

"If we're going fast, how come we're not feeling any, you know, butterflies?" I asked.

"She means g-forces," Lars said. "Why aren't we feeling them if we really are accelerating and moving through atmosphere?"

"We are still in a pocket of shivering space," the Commodore explained, "but the energy requirement is a mere fraction of our intrasolar-system jaunt."

"It's efficient *and* comfortable," Med Tech Tek added, sounding a bit like a dorky advertisement.

Brit was staring at the screen. "It looks like a desert down there."

I could make out hills and rocks of ruddy red and bland pink with subtle tones of brown and beige. "Hey, there's something moving." I pointed to an object in the middle of a rocky field.

A tiny vehicle was inching across the landscape. It had lots of tires and flat square plates like solar panels on the top. We came in closer and closer. The thing looked familiar. I felt like I had seen it on the news.

"It's the Rover," Brit said, "or a simulator."

"Try not to leave a shadow," Med Tech Tek advised. "Shadows always get those NASA transmitters buzzing."

"And dusting off the panels certainly raises a commotion," Citizen Lady added.

At that, they all made the chuckling sound—I checked on Brit; her eyebrows were raised as high as they could go.

"The only Rover I can think of is the one they put on Mars," I said sarcastically.

"Precisely," said the Commodore.

18
Joyful bad order

We passed the supposed Rover and got closer to some boring fields of rock and sand.

"There it is!" Citizen Lady touched the screen and a grid enhanced the area.

I could barely see a little wisp of white vapor. I never would have seen it if Citizen Lady hadn't pointed it out. The craft moved closer to hover right next to the misty "rip."

"We shouldn't get so close," I said. "The cloud behind the garage made us all feel sick."

"This one is exactly the opposite," Citizen Lady said. "Come stand over here."

"Can we leave our square?" I asked.

"Of course. The field-shower is no longer necessary," the Commodore said.

I carefully stuck my foot out, and then Brit and I walked hesitantly forward to stand by the window—or the movie, or whatever it was. Lars and Albert joined us.

"I feel something strange," I said. "Is that feeling coming from the white mist?"

"Indeed it is," Citizen Lady confirmed.

It was as though I had just stepped into a shaken-up soda pop, only the carbonation was made out of thought, and all the thoughts were beautiful and kind and good. They bubbled into my mind and over my skin and made me feel that all was well with the universe and me and just everything.

"Are you in there, Albert?" The way the thoughts bubbled around made me think of Albert's memos.

He sent me a solid message to show that he was Albert, and I was Pearl, and these bubbling thoughts were something else. His memo was happy, yet guarded. He showed me some joyful, bouncing particles that moved with a hyperactivity that wasn't quite right. **Joyful bad order**, he was quick to say.

The happy carbonation lessened and vanished, but the whole experience had put me in a fantastic mood. I noticed that the craft had drifted away from the little white cloud. The Commodore was concentrating again. He must have been steering.

"Did *this* leak start all by itself?" I asked.

"Yes," said Med Tech Tek. "It occurred at the same time as the other. We theorize an entangled response of opposite polarity."

I ignored his mumbo jumbo; I could only take so much. "Why did you bring us *here?*"

"The triad—that is, *we* propose that Albert make some inquiries from this tear, where it is safer."

"You guys are super smart. Why don't *you* do it?"

This caught the Commodore's attention and he answered for all of them. "The triad does not possess the consciousness required for this procedure. We would do it if we could." The SMHR units put on their best regretful faces.

"We propose that Albert's excellent consciousness can slip into the half-constant and return with some answers," said Citizen Lady.

"I don't like the idea of Albert going in there," I objected.

"He would not enter physically—that would cause his demise," Med Tech Tek argued. "He would only send his thoughts to try to find answers."

"Do you even want to try this, Albert?" I asked.

Yes, yes, so fascinating. Albert memoed an example of metal shavings being drawn to a magnet, like that's how much he wanted to try.

"Would he be safe?" I asked. "I mean, there were really scary feelings down at the other rip. Can you guarantee that Albert will be safe?"

The three SMHR units turned toward each other.

Maybe they were talking it over in their heads—or whatever parts communicated.

"The guarantee is not absolute," Citizen Lady acknowledged. "We are dealing with an unknown event."

Albert sent another willful memo. **Must try to fix bad order. Must try. Must try.**

"You are so stubborn," I told him. "Wait . . . what happens if we don't do *anything*? Like, if we put a wall around the cloud in the woods and just stay away from it?"

The three SMHR units all shook their heads. The Commodore stopped watching the wall screen to answer. "The imbalance will only grow and grow until a flood of negatively charged energies saturates your world. All living minds are at risk."

"That's not good," I mumbled, stating the obvious.

Albert sent a memo that claimed he could keep the scary thoughts at bay. He showed me a wall of snow encircling a cartoon Albert. The wall kept the army of red spiders out. With this assurance and with Albert so stoked to help, I decided he might as well attempt it. This problem was bigger than both of us.

"Where're your lasers and the equipment you need to do this?"

"We theorize that because the pressure is mild, Albert can safely slip his inquiries into this end of the tear without the use of invasive equipment *if* he can keep his thoughts neutral—neither positive nor negative. The triad can code his thoughts and direct them with our integral craft." The Commodore stepped aside. "Albert, if you will stand over here?"

19
The thought that rose

Albert heard Pearl say, "Okay, Albert, but if things get weird—get out."

He could sense her worry, born of fear for his well-being.

Albert sent his sister a memo that was unusually sentimental: He made it warm like a sunset, but it was melancholy, too, like the end of a wonderful day. **I must try for our father**, it said.

He and Pearl shared a wistful longing for that brilliant man—the man for whom everything had gone so terribly wrong. Albert wished he could correct his father's legacy. He wished he could erase the blackened memories that tarnished the life and death of Albert Day Sr. Perhaps the only vindication he would receive lay in the heart of his son. Albert was determined to fix this mess to honor his dad, to protect his sister, to help save them all.

Albert walked to the wall-screen that was also a window.

He was so stimulated by the fascinating turn of events and the data that the SMHR units revealed that he could hardly contain himself. He had to concentrate to calm his mind, to focus.

The Commodore motioned for Albert to place his hand on a panel that appeared. Now he was connected to the integral craft, which was ready to code his thoughts and direct them toward the tear. He closed his eyes and sensed the thick cloud of electronic data that the SMHR units and their craft exuded. It was a phenomenon that was similar to thought, only more rigid and mechanical. It was close to consciousness—so very close—and Albert saw where they came up short, but he couldn't explore that now.

He prepared to send a memo that was a general inquiry within a direct channel. He'd done this millions of times, but the fractal element made it more challenging. Albert perceived how the SMHR units had tried and failed, and armed with this new information, he was confident that he would succeed.

He took a deep breath and began to shape his memos into ever smaller fractals, embedding details and questions into the virtual stream that flowed away to the half-constant. But the SMHR craft pulsed and clicked, rejecting the command. Citizen Lady came forward and stood close. Melding with her craft she attempted a number of different configurations, one after another after another . . .

Albert breathed and concentrated, trying to stay on task.

Citizen Lady attempted more than three million configurations without a twitch or movement of any kind— and then she found one that was somewhat compatible with human consciousness, though it was time sensitive and fleeting. If she could just skew the command with a triad override . . . There, now the SMHR craft did its job with a pleasant buzz.

Albert proceeded, keeping his thoughts neutral and calm, imagining the fractals rushing smaller and smaller, slipping into a channel that sent his consciousness to that other place.

He was in! But he had to control both excitement and fear; he had to stay neutral to get answers. Fear might attract joy, and he'd be crushed by an onslaught of thoughts—and the thoughts were everywhere, squeezed into this corner of an unknowable universe. He kept his consciousness as calm as a dull afternoon counting dust particles . . . and he began to sense the thoughts of this measureless world around him. Some were familiar human thoughts, but others were foreign and almost incomprehensible in their structure; they came from curious creatures and strange, faraway worlds. Some were so energetic that they leaked in from the future, and some were fading remnants of staggering antiquity. Some were individual and some were vast conglomerates of a whole. Some were biological and some were . . . something else. But they were all positive and good. They were all happy and hopeful.

Normally, it was easy for Albert to attract the data he desired. Thoughts in his world were as accessible and as easily read as text messages. They were *real*, with their own shape and energy, and when they left for the half-constant, there were always more.

With Pearl, he could communicate comfortably right at the source. Her thoughts were simple and clear and almost as naturally good as the best thoughts that bubbled forth from this tear. Albert was proud of Pearl for that; he couldn't help but be proud. He'd sampled millions upon millions of thoughts, and Pearl's outlook was something special. What's more, she didn't even know it.

But the frenetic, happy thoughts in this space were hard to capture. Their messages to him were brief and disjointed. Though their charges were upbeat and positive, there was something unsettling in this energy as a whole. They lacked something. They needed something. They kept bouncing away in search of it.

Albert's consciousness reached out, trying to get a solid thought or an equation from this crowded world, but informative data evaded him. He'd hoped for answers, but no answers came—at least not in any form he could decipher. The fantastic, buoyant energy just seemed to push him away, until—wait, what was that? Yes, here was something— something he could hold onto. It definitely came from the half-constant, and it was definitely human. The something settled into a pattern that fit itself into words. There was a warm familiarity in the flavor of this thought; it was humble, and sweet—and desperate.

> **Remember I love you and Mary and the baby with all my heart and soul. Please, please remember my love.**

The thought was so powerful that it rose above all the others and made itself known. It ascended and blossomed with astounding will and with a strength that was unfathomable. Despite a sense of wanting to be away, there it stayed for a tiny fraction of a moment, which in quantum terms could have been a billion lifetimes.

There was a sudden flash of white light, and the strange thoughts were gone. The connection had failed. Albert stood in awe, frozen inward. He sent Pearl a brief memo to let her know he was unscathed, and then he reflected on what he'd experienced. He wasn't quite sure what to do with the data he'd gathered, but he did know that it was fascinating and beautiful, and it made him feel wonderful. What were the chances that he could have found *remember my love* in the midst of a universe? It was not a matter of chance that he found his father's thought. This was good order.

20
It's the red spiders

After shivering the space back from wherever the heck we'd been, we took the Volkswagen to Myrtle Road—at least that's where the Commodore said we were going. I still couldn't see anything through the fog, but when the car stopped buzzing, the cold haze cleared, just a little.

"Hey, we're right in front of the house!" I was thrilled to be home, to be back on Myrtle where things were normal. But they weren't really normal, were they?

Outside looked like twilight with night falling fast. I wondered how long we'd been away. Had this fog hung around all day or was it some kind of smoke screen that came out of the Volkswagen? I was beginning to suspect the latter.

The atmosphere of twilight and deep snow and the unusual fog gave the end of the road a mysterious feel. Everything felt a little off.

"What are we going to tell my mom?" I asked.

The Commodore was in the driver's seat; the other two SMHR units had stayed back at "the lab."

"I took the liberty of scanning the location of the Ma and the Meemaw," the Commodore said.

The Ma and the Meemaw? Brit mouthed.

"The inclement weather has caused an accident on the highway number 266," he continued. "This has impeded their progress. They will update you on the telephone-recorder."

"Are they okay?" Normally, nothing impeded the progress of my mother and grandmother.

"They are in good health and were not involved in the traffic mishap," he assured me. "But the highway number 266 is blocked by a large freight conveyance, as well as many small vehicles. It would appear that vehicular ground travel is doubtful."

There was a quiet pause that sat heavy in the air.

"Mr. Commodore, what do we do now—I mean about the rip and the imbalance and all?" I asked.

"Follow Albert's lead," he instructed. "Albert is the key. He will be processing the information he received today."

I figured Albert was very distracted because he hadn't sent me any memos since he'd assured me he was "unscathed." He'd just stared at the screens all the way back from Mars. Yeah, he was processing.

"The triad will return tomorrow," the Commodore said. "With eyeballs, of course." He bobbed his head and the doors of the Volkswagen sprang open.

"Goodbye," he said abruptly.

"But, Mr. Commodore—"

"Goodbye," he said again. He waved his silly, four-fingered wave. There was nothing else to do but leave.

Me and Brit and Albert and Lars bumbled out of the car. Lars went first, stomping a trail through the snow to the house.

"I'm starving," Lars said. "You guys realize we haven't eaten all day? Or has it been more than one day?" He turned to check on the rest of us. "Man, that little car is quiet for an old V-Dub. I didn't even hear it leave."

I looked behind me. The Volkswagen was gone. I retraced my steps to the road. "There're no tire tracks," I said. "No tracks coming or going." Instead, the snow had melted in a round circle where the car had been parked.

Lars and Brit had followed me over, and now we were all staring at the melted circle.

"Yeah, I don't think it was a Volkswagen," I muttered. "With no tracks, there's nowhere to go but *up*."

All three of us stared upward. The fog was thinning and I thought maybe we'd see a hovering Volkswagen, ridiculous as that seemed. But there was nothing up there.

"Hey! You hoodlums get off my street!"

It was Mrs. Wagner, wearing Mr. Wagner's work jacket. She was standing on her porch with her gray hair sticking out all crazy—and she was pointing a rifle at us! It was her husband's prize repeating rifle, a beautiful antique that he kept displayed above his fireplace. "Get off my street!" she shrieked again.

"Mrs. Wagner, it's me, Mary!" I was shocked by her behavior. She was normally such a nice neighbor, and she always handed out really good treats on Halloween. "You know Brit and Lars—are you all right?" Her eyes kept darting around and she was flinching like something was about to get her. *About to get her*. Oh, no.

"No I'm not all right!" Her voice sounded high-pitched and scary. "Nothin's right!"

Mr. Wagner came out on the porch, moving carefully. He had a black eye. "Now, Lois, they're just kids. I want you to put that gun down and come inside."

"Ken, I don't feel so good. I don't feel like myself." Mrs. Wagner rubbed her forehead and she looked like she might cry.

"I know. Now, come along. Quit frightening these children." Mr. Wagner gently took the rifle and put his arm on her back, trying to guide her without spooking her.

Mrs. Wagner paused and turned around. "I'm sorry,

Mary. I—I'm not myself." And then she stepped into the house, leaving her husband on the porch.

"Mr. Wagner, was Mrs. Wagner in the woods?" I moved closer to hear his response.

"Yeah, she was looking for Ed Shinn because those goats of his were raising such a ruckus. Lois was going to go feed them and—well, she came back to the house just fighting mad, over nothing. Look at this—" he pointed to the black eye—"she took a swing at me!" Quietly he added, "I put some sedatives in her tea. In all our years, I have never seen her like this."

"I think you did the right thing," I told him. "Try to get her to rest. And take care of yourself, Mr. Wagner. Maybe some ibuprofen will keep that eye from swelling."

"Thanks, Mary, I will. I don't know what got into her . . . " He went back in the house and closed the door softly.

"Wow," Brit exclaimed. "I can't believe that Lois Wagner would smack old Ken like that. They always seemed to really like each other."

"They still do. It's the red spiders," I whispered.

"The what?"

"Something that Albert said about the red mist. Come on, let's get in the house."

21
A sour taste

I made a beeline to the phone. The rooms were cold, as usual, because Ma wouldn't turn the heat up over 65 degrees. She said gas was too expensive, plus we had a good woodstove and a bunch of firewood that she'd gotten from Bob Dietz. She'd traded eight quarts of her home-canned plum chutney for that wood. I think that we got the better end of that deal.

"I'll start a fire," Lars said. He headed back outside to the wood pile.

"Thanks, Lars!" I called. I clicked on the message button which was flashing an insistent red eye.

"Hi kids!" It was Ma's cheerful voice. I was so happy to hear her. It made me feel more grounded, more like myself. Ma had sort of a low voice and it was full of humor that only she and I understood.

"You won't believe the excitement we've had. A big tanker jackknifed on 266, and a bunch of cars plowed into each other. No one is hurt but the road is a mess! I was thinking that it might take a while, so I pulled a U-ey and scooted back downtown. I got a hold of Bob and he said the road won't open for hours, so Meemaw and I went to Rona Zucker's and—what's that?—oh, Rona says she's got cabin fever and she's thrilled to have the company. Anyhow, Meemaw is tired and cold and—what's that?—oh, Meemaw says she's not tired, she's just mad that the road is closed. We're going to stay for supper; Rona's making meatloaf, and Bob promised he'd call the minute the road opens. Now, Mary, you see that Brit stays over, and in fact, ask if Lars will come hang out for a while. I'd feel better about—well, I'd feel better. There's that pizza in the freezer. It's three-o-clock right now. Call me."

Brit had already found the pizza and was reading the instructions. Lars was clunking around in the front room, making a fire. Albert had gone to the bathroom—I heard the toilet flush. It seemed like the day hadn't really happened.

"Did we really go to Mars?" I asked, looking for general confirmation.

"We went *somewhere*," Lars said from the front room. The fire was starting to crackle.

"Yeah, we definitely went somewhere," Brit repeated.

"Lars, didn't you put that ID on the table?" I asked.

"Right in the middle."

"Well, it's not there."

"That Commodore guy probably palmed it." Brit scowled. "Mary, what did you mean by *red spiders?*"

"It was how Albert explained those bad feelings that came from the mist. I think he meant that the bad stuff could get into your head like spiders."

"*Eww.* And you think that's what happened to Mrs. Wagner?"

"That's what the Commodore said would happen. And it's only going to get worse with more negative stuff flooding in. I mean, it made all of us feel pretty rotten."

"And I bet it makes the animals feel rotten, too." Brit clenched her jaw with this grim realization.

I pictured the coyote and the birds. From what all we'd learned from the SMHR units, the odd behavior that we'd witnessed seemed much more menacing. I felt my stomach twist and it gave my mouth a sour taste. "I gotta eat something."

Brit and I had finally changed out of our pajamas and put on our jeans and big sweaters. We sat down to gobble the pizza with Lars, and we were downing big glasses of water, too. I guess we were all dehydrated.

"Albert!" I yelled. "Come and eat!" He'd gone to lie down while I talked to Ma on the phone. I'd tried to reassure her that all was well here at home. And she tried to reassure me that she was having a great time at Rona Zucker's.

I hadn't gotten a single memo from Albert. He'd seemed tired and unsociable. I hoped he was okay.

"Lars, that's four pieces. You're eating way more than your share," Brit accused.

"I'm bigger than you are," Lars replied with a droll expression.

"So, Lars, do you mind sticking around? My mom thought it would be a good idea, with Mr. Shinn and all—"

BOOM! There was a blast from outside.

22
A horrible place

The three of us froze, looking at each other across the table.

"Do you think—oh my God, I hope that's not Mrs. Wagner," Brit said.

"I'll go see." Lars rushed outside and ran into the snowy street. Brit and I watched him from the open door.

Mr. Wagner was out on his porch, staring at the woods—he must have heard it, too.

"Mr. Wagner, is Mrs. Wagner in the house?" Lars called.

"Yes, she's sleeping!" he hissed. "And I want her to *keep* sleeping."

"Where's Albert?" I asked.

"I haven't seen him since you called your mom," Brit said.

There was a flash of a memo that appeared in my head. For a half second I saw red spiders swarming on a dirty plaid hat. The sense that came with it was one of danger, and something like . . . tragedy. Now it was panic that twisted my gut.

"Albert?" I called. I ran to his room. "He's not in here!"

"Check the bathroom," Brit said.

BOOM! It was a gunshot, all right. It came from the woods, I was sure.

"He's not in the bathroom!"

I hurried through Meemaw's room and hurtled off the back porch, slogging through the deep snow that filled our backyard. I was running as fast as I could.

"Albert!" I called.

BOOM! The gun cracked again.

Night had fallen, clear and crisp. The light from the porch was reflecting off the snow. It looked like a Christmas card, but it didn't feel that way. I entered the woods, straining my eyes to find Mr. Shinn. I yelled out even though I couldn't see him. "Mr. Shinn, quit shooting! You've got neighbors, for Chrissake!"

"Stay away!" the old man bellowed. "Albert, you get your butt back home and don't you come out here again." He sounded angry, desperate.

I saw Albert's unmoving silhouette on the trail, and I realized with dreadful clarity that the reason I could see my brother so well was because of the backdrop of glowing, red mist. The dangerous cloud had grown from a basketball shape to the size of a car, and whatever bad vibe the mist was spewing was already making me sick.

"Mr. Shinn, please quit shooting," I begged. "You might hurt Albert!"

Albert memoed for me to **GO HOME**.

Right, like I would leave him. He looked so small standing there, backlit by the broiling red.

"I know where I'm aiming," Mr. Shinn shouted—"at that devil mist. It's bad, I tell you. It's evil."

BOOM! Another shot resounded. The car-size sphere of mist wobbled and grew larger.

"You are making it worse!" I cried.

"I'll give that thing what for." Mr. Shinn crossed the wire and ran crazily right toward the blood-red cloud.

Albert ran after him. He made a clumsy interception, tackling Mr. Shinn by lunging at his leg. The old man stumbled and went face-down in the snow. They were too close—far too close to the anomaly. They must have been paralyzed with horrible thoughts. Mr. Shinn kicked Albert away and managed to right himself.

To our horror, the old man raised the gun to his head, and pulled the trigger as he leapt into the mist. He vanished, and the atmosphere made a sickening wave, like airborne vertigo. Now the angry mist was the size of a house.

Lars was trying to push past me to grab Albert. But

something told me that Lars couldn't handle *this*. The bad thoughts would ruin him, just like they ruined poor Mr. Shinn. I could do it, I was sure. I just had to keep my mind clean and sparse like a quiet yard surrounded by a tidy wall of snow.

"It's got to be *me*, Lars. I can handle it. I've had lots of practice with Albert."

"But I've had lots of practice with rotten people," Lars said.

"That won't protect you, Lars."

Albert was maybe twenty feet ahead of me on the trail, sprawled in the snow where he'd fallen. He wasn't moving. I could feel the mean thoughts trying to sting me, scrambling around my mind like busy, scratching spiders. They wanted in.

I halted Lars in his tracks with my hand. "Back up," I commanded, as if he were a big dog. He stumbled back, away from the mist.

I took a deep breath, filling my mind with a clean bubble of snow-white silence, and I moved forward to get my brother. Down the trail, around a log, stomping through the deep snow into the cloud of red. I stooped and got a good grip on Albert's hand, and I began to drag him away from the vile mist. I tried to keep my mind full of icy calm, so full there'd be no room for anything else. There was just my thought-bubble of clean, white snow, frozen in my mind's eye—until a lone red spider scuttled through.

23
Come back!

In a smoky red haze, I pictured the triad; the monsters with no eyes. They had tricked me into all this, and who knew what their motives were? Evil aliens from an evil galaxy. And Albert . . . he'd gone along with their conspiracy. He'd communicated with the half-constant before he was even born. What kind of monster was *he*?

I felt sick and disgusted with everyone around me. Brit probably thought she was so much smarter than I was, but look where she lived. Look at her pitiful mom, and look at Lars with his lame job and his slacker friends. What a bunch of losers. Even Ma—still angry at her crazy, dead husband after eight long years, and making the worst wage ever at the school district! And why was her mother still living with us? Meemaw acting like a dumb, foul-mouthed hick living in our stupid laundry room. Four people in that tiny dump with a leaky roof. What a pathetic life!

When I thought about myself, it was with this sinking

feeling, like I was drowning in insecurity about how I looked, and how stupid I was—like I could try and try with all my might, and I would never dig out of this pit. And why dig out, anyhow? The world was a rotten place, inhabited by rotten people, and I was just one more.

Stop it! I screamed inside my mind. I forced the clean bubble into place; as cool and clean as snow, like a sigh, like a breeze from the mountains. It was too cold in my mind for the spiders, and far too calm for their liking.

I realized I'd dragged Albert all the way back to the front door. Lars and Brit had been trying to help, but I hadn't even noticed. Albert was sending me a message. It was faint, but it was growing: **Good thoughts, Pearl. Come back!** I saw a picture in my head: an iridescent pearl shining to the farthest edges of space.

I began to cry and I think I was slapping my head with my hands. I think I was clawing my hair until Brit stopped me. She and Lars held my arms so I couldn't hurt myself. I'd gone to such a horrible place.

Oh, God, I was so grateful to be home.

Lars was sitting on the rug contemplating the last triangle of pizza. Brit brought me another glass of water. "Thanks, Brit," I mumbled.

I was sitting on the footstool next to the woodstove. Under my feet was the nubby hook rug with antique roses on it. Ma loved that rug. She'd found it at a yard sale and was so happy to get it for five bucks. "See?" she'd said excitedly. "You don't have to be rich to surround yourself with beauty." Ma was so right.

Over there was our lumpy brown sofa, next to the recliner that Meemaw always sat in. We kept a cover on it because the arm was duct-taped. It was sort of a piece of crap, but I loved it. It smelled like Meemaw and her awful cigarettes. Meemaw, with her sharp wisdom and her loyalty that was absolute.

The amber glow from the little stove was pretty on the hardwood floor. It made the room seem warmer than it was—way warmer than outside where snow swirled around an evil mist. My house was good and solid, and the wood box was full because Lars had thought to fill it. And I had a glass of water, here, because Brit had thought to bring it. You don't have to be rich to surround yourself with beauty.

I stared at the glass of water in my hand.

"It was awful," I said in a dry, little voice. "The way the mist made me feel . . . I was so hopeless and mean."

"I got a taste of it," Brit said. "I don't know how you escaped."

"I could feel it trying to get me," Lars said. "I shouldn't

have let you go, Mary. I was chicken."

"No! It would have wrecked you. There's a mind trick to keeping it out, but I couldn't do it for very long, even with Albert's memos."

Some of the sickening thoughts came back to me and I was ashamed; the mean stuff I'd thought about my Ma and Meemaw, about Brit and Lars and Albert. . . .

"I wish I could scrub out my brain!" I squeezed my head and ran my fingers through my hair. "Then I wouldn't have to think about what a jerk-wad I am."

"That's *not* who you are," Brit said. "You are nice, and don't you forget it. It was the mist that filled your head with bad and negative stuff."

"I don't know—it was like the mist brought out the worst possible me. I mean everyone has happy and good thoughts, and everyone has gloomy and bummer thoughts, but the mist wrecked all that was good, and it triggered all that was bad. Like it was hungry for good stuff, only when it found it, it changed it."

What I *didn't* tell Brit and Lars was that I could picture what the mist might do to a big group of people. It would be the worst kind of craziness—like angry zombies in real life. I shuddered.

"This is bad," Lars said. "If we call the police or the army or something, then those people would be in danger—and anyhow, activity just makes it worse. I mean even the snowballs revved it up, and then when Shinn killed himself. . . . "

"Where do you suppose he went?" Brit said. "The SMHRs said the half-constant couldn't support human life."

"Well, he was a dead duck," I pointed out. "But you know what? I think he was trying to protect us. And I think maybe that's what happened to my dad. I think he was infected eight years ago, and he could feel it getting to him. Maybe he ran his car into that bulkhead on purpose because in a crazy way he was trying to protect us, just like poor old Mr. Shinn."

"That sort of breaks my heart," Brit said.

There was a sad pause while we thought about the sacrifices of others—but the sadness morphed into an overwhelming sense of the terrible trouble we were in.

"What do we do now?" I asked. "I mean, this is huge."

"We need to do what the Commodore told us to do," Lars said firmly, like he was trying to be calm and logical. "We need to follow Albert's lead."

The three of us turned to look at my brother. He was curled up on the couch, eyes open, thinking.

Brit shivered all over. "Either I'm nervous or it's cold in here."

"It's cold," I confirmed. "I think I left the back door open—" when all of a sudden I got a tense memo from

Albert that said **Complications**, coupled with what looked like a shiny, black shoe.

There was an assertive *bang-bang-bang* on the front door.

Lars walked over and stood there. "Who is it?" he demanded.

"FBI," a man's voice said.

24
The men from BETI

Lars turned the front porch light on and we peered out the window. There were two men standing there in black police-type jackets with matching caps.

"What do you want?" Lars asked.

"We'd like to ask you some questions," the taller man said.

Lars looked back at me with his hands open.

"Albert, what do you think?" I asked. After all, we were supposed to be *following Albert's lead*.

He memoed a combo-message involving the black shoe and a feeling that the shoe was necessary—**LET THEM IN** was the conclusion.

I shrugged. "Let them in."

Lars opened the door, and the two men stepped into our living room. One was very tall and trim—the other was short and muscular. The short guy smiled and seemed friendly. His tall partner was all business.

"I'm Agent Saunders," the tall one said. He was a clean-shaven black man with close-cropped hair. The whites of his eyes, and his teeth, and his crisp, white collar were all gleaming with health and cleanliness. I found it hard to pull my eyes away. He flipped a badge too quickly for me to really see it. Then he tipped his head toward the other man. "This is my partner, Agent Guy."

Brit and I couldn't help it. We found each other's eyes and raised our brows. I knew she was thinking, "*Secret Agent Guy.*" I tried not to smile.

Albert sent me a memo that said **Not FBI. They are BETI.**

I stared at Albert, willing him to tell me more.

Albert elaborated with a picture of a blipping screen and a noise like radar from an old movie. **Bureau**—blip. **Extra**-blip. **Terrestrial**—blip. **Investigation**.

"We've gotten some complaints about suspicious activity in your neighborhood," Agent Saunders said. "Perhaps you saw an unusual—uh—vehicle? And of course those gunshots."

I figured I'd stay close to the truth. "Yes, there was a strange car parked at the turnaround, an old V-Dub Bug. And not too long ago we heard gunshots."

"Where'd they come from?" he asked.

"It's hard to say. The snow makes things all muffled," I answered.

Agent Guy interrupted. "Saunders, I'm going to take a look around the house and check the backyard. You talk to the kids—and don't scare them." He winked at us, which was reassuring. "When I come back, maybe you could rustle me up a cup of coffee—I didn't get my usual because Saunders here wouldn't stop." He grinned like this was just hilarious. "This partner of mine refuses to go through the drive-through."

"I know how to make coffee, Agent Guy. I could make you some," I offered.

Agent Guy was smiling like he didn't have a care in the world—unlike grumpy Saunders. "I'll take you up on that," the short agent said. His face was pink from the cold, and he looked very young, like he was fresh from the academy, or maybe he just had a baby face. Agent Guy flipped his collar higher and scrunched his hat down, preparing to go back outside. He gave Saunders a tiny nod, and then he left, closing the door behind him.

Saunders stood there awkwardly. It seemed to me that Saunders didn't really like kids, yet he was the one who stayed behind to talk to us. It was like they chose the wrong guy for the interview—or maybe they were trying to psych us out, like a mean cop versus nice cop head game. That's how they did it in the movies.

"Are you Mary Day?" Agent Saunders finally asked.

"Yes, I am."

"And is that your brother, Albert?" He gestured toward the couch.

"Yes, that's him."

"And what are *your* names?" he said, turning to Brit and Lars.

"I'm Brit Stickle," Brit answered.

"And I'm her brother, Lars. We live nearby."

"I'd like to speak to your parents." Agent Saunders was looking at *me*.

"Well, my dad is dead, but you probably know that because you already know our names. And my mom's not here. She's stuck in Adeline. They closed the road."

"So it's just you kids here alone?"

The fact that Agent Saunders said he was FBI when he wasn't, and he knew our names when he shouldn't, and now he was pointing out how *alone* we were—well, it all gave me the creeps.

"Of course we're not alone," I lied. "Our uncle is staying with us. He just went out to check the neighborhood after hearing those gunshots. Agent Guy will probably run into him."

"And who is your uncle?"

"Uncle Commodore," I said, trying to sound sincere. "He'll be back any minute."

"Uncle Commodore, huh?" Agent Saunders suppressed

a smirk. Then he froze and cocked his head slightly, concentrating. From this new angle, I spied the device in his ear; he was wearing an earpiece.

"What do you mean *a mist*?" he said, talking into the air.

"Copy that," he snapped. "You kids wait here." Saunders turned toward the door.

It was then that the realization slammed me—Agent Guy had gone into the woods! If he was close enough to see the mist, he was already in trouble. Why didn't I stop him?

"Don't go outside," I blurted. "It's not safe!"

"I'll decide what is safe, Miss Day. Now I suggest you lock your doors and wait here. And maybe give your *Uncle Commodore* a call and tell him to get his tail back here."

At that very moment—at the end of "*get his tail back here*"—the landline rang.

25
The bad was getting worse

Agent Sanders narrowed his eyes. "I'll get it," he said.

"Hello? Yes, this is Saunders. And how do you know that—*who is this*?"

Agent Saunders listened a little longer. Then he hung up the phone.

"Who was it?" I asked.

"Apparently it was your *Uncle Commodore*. Do you have an attic?"

"Yeah, but it's tiny." I tipped my head to the ceiling in the hall. "And we have to pull the ladder thingy down."

"Let's go," Saunders said, heading for the hall. He jumped and easily grabbed the handle that opened the hinged trap door, and then he pulled down the folding ladder. "Come on, kids. Hustle."

"Are you serious? Why should we go up there?" I asked.

"Because your Uncle Commodore said so."

Albert went first, moving unusually fast. I followed Albert, and Brit followed me. Lars was stepping up, but he hesitated and turned around.

"Are you coming?" he asked Saunders.

Agent Saunders didn't answer right away. It was like he couldn't decide.

Albert sent me a memo that said **Hurry, Saunders, life is good**—there was a happy sun and a warm feeling that went with it. **The Commodore knows**, Albert added.

"We need you up *here*," I said in a whiny voice. I figured if I sounded pathetic he'd be stoked to protect us.

That seemed to help him come to a decision. He scurried up the ladder and closed the hatch.

A pale light filtered in from the small window at the gable. I could see the silhouettes of Lars and Agent Saunders hunching way over because even at its peak the ceiling was less than five feet. Agent Saunders accidentally kicked a bucket that had been placed to catch leaks. It made a metallic *clankity* racket; luckily it had no water inside.

We stood there in the darkness, balanced on the two-by-sixes—in between the joists was just insulation and plaster and anybody's foot could have gone through the ceiling. Albert sent me a cottony memo that said **HUSH.**

"*Shh*," I whispered, and just as I did, an odd sound came from the porch—*pew-pew-pew!*

"I know you're in there, Saunders," a deep voice said. "You set me up, buddy-boy. You think I'm stupid? You sent me into the woods to face that thing. Well I'm one step ahead of you, *partner*." The man's voice was oily with hatred.

"Who is that?" I said in an almost-silent whisper.

"It sounds like my partner," Saunders whispered back. "But it can't be him—he would never say those things."

The Partner was below us in the hall. *Pew, pew, pew*. The same muffled impacts resounded—was he shooting with a silencer? He must have lost it, big time. I knew firsthand how suspicious and angry the mist could make you feel, but this poor agent had turned so quickly, so completely. The cruel thoughts must have taken him by surprise, and the bad was getting worse.

Agent Saunders found my hand and squeezed it. Maybe he wasn't a total jerk. I found Albert's hand and squeezed that, and he didn't resist. I sensed a rustle. Saunders was quietly taking something from inside his coat. I could see the silhouette of a gun.

The Partner was near the bathroom now. *Pew, pew!* *Crash*! He kicked a door open.

"Saunders, are you in there, old pal?"

I heard more movement; the sudden metallic scrape as he whipped the shower curtain open. Then he was back in the hall, trying to tread softly. But the thing about our house was that it was old, and just about every floorboard creaked.

He was heading for the laundry room where the back door was open. Maybe he would see our footprints in the snow. Maybe he would think we had run to the woods to hide, and he'd follow our trail and get the heck out of here. But no, he'd already seen them when he went out to investigate. I'll bet it was our footprints that led him to the red mist in the first place.

These were the thoughts running through my head when a bright light filled the backyard. It illuminated the attic, too, and I could see shock on the faces of each crouching comrade. The light was bluish-white and pulsing with a luminosity that almost hurt my eyes. It seemed to come from above.

"What the—?" It was the Partner's voice—now he was outside. "It's them!" he shouted. "Saunders, it's the—" *Pew-pew-pew.* Ole trigger-finger was shooting again. Then silence.

"What's going on out there?" I squeaked.

Agent Saunders's earpiece made a horrible, static scrape, and we all flinched. He grabbed it out of his ear.

From the earpiece came another round of static and then a polite voice said, "So sorry, Agent Saunders. We had to subdue your partner as he was quite irrational. It's safe now."

I let out a huge exhale of relief. "That's Mr.—um, I mean, that's my Uncle Commodore," I said.

Agent Saunders shook his head. "Let's get out of here."

We took turns climbing down the ladder. As I was heading down, Albert showed me the image of a silly four-fingered wave. The three SMHR units were around here somewhere.

Albert was the last one to climb down. I was helping him place his foot when I heard a shuffle on the porch and a creaking floorboard. The front door was still ajar from the Partner's assault.

Agent Saunders put his arms out and hissed, "Get down!" And then he pulled his sidearm and pointed it at the door.

26
Uncle Commodore and friends

▌t's okay," I told Saunders. "I'm pretty sure it's just Uncle
▌Commodore and his, um, friends."

Agent Saunders glowered. "Back up and stay low," he
directed. He even made Lars duck down under his bossy
glare.

At the edge of the door, and with his gun ready, he said,
"Who's there?"

"The Com—er—Uncle Commodore, of course. And
Citizen Lady and Med Tech Tek. Agent Saunders, time is of
the essence. Cease your posturing and let us in."

Saunders cracked open the door a bit more. He stared at
the SMHR units for a few seconds and then pushed the door
open. Grudgingly, he stepped aside.

"What happened to my partner?" he asked.

"He's unconscious for now, by the refuse containers,"
said the Commodore.

"I've worked with that man for three years, and *that* was *not* my partner." Saunders shook his head in guarded disbelief. "What happened to him?"

"He was not himself, as you surmise," the Commodore answered. "He was infected with a dangerous quantity of the, er, *mist*. Most regrettable."

"Was it *your* craft that BETI was tracking?" Saunders asked, this time not bothering to lie.

The Commodore didn't bother to lie, either. "Indeed it was. When the probability of injury to the children became a certainty, we swooped in to make a physical intercept."

"And just what are you doing in those woods?" Saunders demanded. "Did one of your crafts go down? Is that what's causing the poisonous mist?"

"Certainly *not*." Citizen Lady was losing her cool. "That," she said, pointing in the direction of the woods, "is why we are breaking protocol and interfering." She shook her head and rolled her eyes. "By rolling these, I am demonstrating *exasperation*."

"Hey, you have eyes!" I said. "They look great."

Citizen Lady seemed pleased. Her new eyes were a pretty shade of purple—an interesting choice with her fair complexion and plastic-yellow hair.

Saunders ignored the fact that I just complimented Citizen Lady on having eyes. "If you and your craft aren't responsible for that mist, what is?"

136

"It's the interdimensional leak," the Commodore said. His new eyes were an odd color of blue, almost turquoise, glinting sharply in the middle of his pale, melon-shaped head.

"Negative thought-energies are seeping into this universe at an alarming rate," the Commodore explained. "They are like poison to the living. Your partner was dangerously altered—and he is but one of billions of life forms in this world. It is most distressing."

"We SMHR units collect and transmit data," Med Tech Tek piped up. His new eyes were a deep gray color that reminded me of storm clouds. "We registered the imbalance and grew alarmed when we studied it further. This anomaly is bad order," he said, using Albert's description. "Agent Saunders, you must call your BETI cohorts and beg them to avoid contact."

I realized, then, that I was hearing the *rattity-tat* of helicopters in the distance.

"He's right," Lars said. "Agent Saunders, you've got to keep your people away from the mist. They'll go crazy if it touches them. Plus, it seems like if anything makes physical contact, then even *more* violent stuff leaks out."

Saunders nodded. With a hand to his ear he said, "Abort NBC. Reassessment is critical. Repeat—abort NBC."

"What is that, like, a TV channel?" I asked.

Saunders frowned, distracted. "It's for Nuclear, Biological, and Chemical recovery."

"You don't want to recover that stuff. It's horrible," I said.

Brit lowered her brows and her eyes became cautious and hard. "I know what that means—these government guys thought that the SMHR units crash-landed in the woods. They wanted to snag some technology."

"We saw them on an ultraviolet scan and tracked them," Saunders confirmed. "Plus satellite detected the mist and—you know it's in our best interest to watch who's coming and going in our airspace, and besides—" Saunders stopped short, listening again to his earpiece. "Yes ma'am. I know but their mother is in the town and—hold on." The tall agent squared his jaw. "I'm going to see if I can get you kids to that town where your mother is staying. Just a moment." Saunders tilted his head as he listened to the voice in his earpiece. Then he turned and walked to the dining room to hear it better—or to get privacy.

Quietly, Brit said, "I don't think they're going to let us go."

Lars moved in closer to hear. "Why do you say that?" he whispered.

"These FBI guys are treating all this like it's some kind of alien contact event."

"They aren't even FBI!" I said softly. "Albert told me they're from some organization called BETI, which stands for Bureau of Extraterrestrial Investigation."

Brit was grim and certain. "I think they're going to haul

us off and, like, hose us down and do tests and stuff. It'll only waste time."

Albert heartily agreed. I know because he sent me a memo that said **Equationaut's guess is true. We should run**. He must have sent a memo to the SMHR units, too, because all three of them were nodding in perfect unison.

In the dining room, Agent Saunders said, "Copy that." But his tone was irritated and his face showed a fleeting shadow of something like frustration or anger.

To the SMHR units he posed a question that sounded a little too casual. "I don't suppose I could persuade you three visitors to come talk to our scientists about your theories on physics, could I?"

"Don't be ridiculous," Citizen Lady said sharply. "We have important work to do. We are not here to favor one culture over another with our technology."

Med Tech Tek agreed with an exaggerated scowl.

Saunders didn't push it. "Well, you kids get your jackets on and we'll go find your mother." When he said the word *mother*, he looked down. I felt like he was lying.

"Okay," I agreed. "Our coats are in Meemaw's room. I put them in the dryer."

Albert led the way down the hall. Once we were in the laundry room, I shut the door just enough so that Saunders couldn't see us. Albert sent me a memo that confirmed

Brit's suspicions. It showed the four of us in a cage.

I could hear Citizen Lady talking to Saunders about ultraviolet detection and the technology of the BETI force. I think she was trying to distract him.

"Everyone have their jacket? Let's go," Lars whispered, and we all bolted off the porch and into the snowy yard, where, incredibly, the SMHR units had parked their "Volkswagen." The vehicle was glowing slightly, and every few seconds the light wobbled and did a crazy trick of illumination that made the car look exactly like a flying saucer.

"Run for the Volkswagen!" Lars ordered. And we ran.

27
Way up

Lights came at us from every direction until the house and the yard and the street were bright as day. The whole neighborhood was crawling with BETI personnel! Some were dressed like the hazardous-materials guys from the movie *E.T.* in bulky, head-to-toe coveralls with protective helmets.

"Get in and lock the doors!" Lars yelled.

Brit stumbled in the snow so Albert and I grabbed her and dragged her to the car. The BETI guys were moving in on us from the front of the house and from over by the garbage cans. I could see the Partner slumped in the snow, his head against a trash can, still unconscious, or worse. We jumped into the Volkswagen, Lars in front, and me and Albert and Brit in the back. Out of the corner of my eye, I saw Agent Saunders in hot pursuit. He was almost to the car, but it was hard for him to run in that snow; he had on those dumb shoes that had no tread. He started to slip. I shut and locked the door just as he skidded into the side of the car. The tall agent smacked the window in frustration, then he darted around to the other side trying to get in the passenger door but Lars had already locked it. The SMHRs had left the engine running; I recognized the hum. Lars shifted into first.

The same incredibly thick fog that had insulated the cul-de-sac earlier in the day returned. It puffed and billowed, obscuring the big lights that the BETI guys were using.

"Go, Lars!" Brit screeched.

"I'm punching it but nothing's happening. Dang it! I can't see a thing."

The car buzzed louder.

"I'll put it in second, but I'm not getting any traction," he said, mostly to himself.

THWACK! We all jumped when a palm slapped the window glass on the front passenger side. "Help!" a muffled voice cried out. "Kids, you gotta let me in!" It was Agent Saunders.

"Sorry, Saunders," I said. "Brit thinks you BETI guys are going to, like, detain us, and we've got research to do."

Brit nodded and gave me an approving look.

There was a *clunk* and a scraping noise from the outside the car.

"Saunders, just let go or you're gonna get hurt!" I yelled.

"If I let go, I'll die!" he yelled back. "We're *way* up."

"It's probably a trick," Lars said, "but I don't want the guy to get hurt. Brit, roll down the window and see what's going on."

Brit climbed over the seat to the front and cranked the chrome window handle. She rolled it down all the way and a blast of snow and frozen air rushed in. A cold-knuckled Saunders grabbed the rim of the door and his other hand reached for the side. "Help me," he begged. I rolled down *my* window and stuck my head out. Saunders was actually *hanging* there. I caught a glimpse of something through the fog—searchlights!—far, far below.

"What?—How?—Agent Saunders, what are you doing?" I asked, which come to think of it, was sort of a dumb question.

"Hanging on!" he barked.

"Kick your legs up!" I shouted.

He obeyed and kicked up a foot, which I grabbed. Bit by bit he managed to scoot his legs in through the window. Once, he slipped, and was hanging by his knees, arms dangling toward the frozen ground so many deadly feet below.

With a last burst of strength, he threw his body up so he was sitting on the window rim, and then he slithered inside until he was sitting on Albert's lap and mine. It was pretty awkward.

I felt his fingers; they were like frozen hotdogs. "You sure got cold out there," I said, pointing out the obvious. I rubbed his hands briskly, trying to warm them up.

From the front seat, Lars said, "Sorry, Saunders, I didn't realize your predicament."

"You know how to drive this thing?" Saunders asked.

"Well, I know how to drive a stick. I didn't exactly expect this kind of performance. Who'd a thought we'd gain so much elevation?" Lars gave a little half-grin.

"Pretty good for this make and model," Saunders said with the tiniest of smirks.

"Normally, I'm not a huge fan of German cars," Lars returned.

"Nor am I," Saunders agreed.

Their wry car talk was interrupted—again—by the noisy *SCHRAAUCH!* from Saunders's earpiece.

"Holy sh—shiplap!" Saunders cried, snatching the device out of his ear.

All I could think about was *holy shiplap*, which made me want to giggle, but I appreciated his effort to not swear in front of us.

From the earpiece we could hear a tinny refrain. "Agent Saunders, the Commodore here. Please direct young Lars to pick us up at these coordinates."

At once, a rectangle on the dashboard lit up with numbers.

"What do I do, Commodore?" Lars yelled.

Saunders was holding the earpiece and pointing it toward Lars. A scratchy-sounding Commodore said, *"Drive."*

Lars put the thing in fourth and "drove." Our view was still choked by the fog which seemed to be following us. We couldn't see where we were and Lars was just driving blind. We were all shocked when something went *THUMP*! on the windshield and black feathers exploded. We'd collided with a crow, and the poor bird slid down the glass and then fell off to one side.

"Oh, man," Brit said. "Lars, watch out for birds!"

"I would, Brit, if I could see anything at all," Lars said testily.

28
Driving to Adeline

The little car hummed in my temples; otherwise, there was no sound.

"Hey Saunders, how come you won't go through the drive-through?" I figured I'd throw some conversation out there.

"I don't like to sit in the line, and I don't like those little windows."

"Little windows?" Brit sounded like she was on the verge of a giggle.

"I don't trust little windows, okay?" He frowned and shifted his position, pulling at his collar like it was suddenly too tight.

"Okay," Brit said.

"And I don't like coffee. Agent Guy drinks way too much of it and he messes up the car. He's always talking and joking and sloshing his coffee everywhere."

"You like things tidy, don't you, Saunders?" I deduced.

He wouldn't answer me. After a few minutes he said, "Agent Guy was a good partner. Probably the best I ever had."

I felt bad about my comment. He'd been complaining about coffee and a messy car because he was worried. The Partner had been his wingman, and now he was crazy—or maybe he was dead. I took Saunders's hand again and gave him a pat. He just gazed out the window but I could have sworn his eyes got watery.

A bass undertone reverberated and joined in harmony with the droning buzz—and then it was silent. The fog thinned. We had stopped, and we seemed to be in downtown Adeline in the parking lot behind the Senior Center. It was dark out, but the activity sign was bright. It said Steak Night and 1-Buck Bingo, only there was hardly anybody in the lot. Probably all the seniors had stayed home because of the bad weather.

"Saunders, please don't call your BETI pals—not yet," Brit said. She had turned around to face him from the front seat. "You need to know what's going on."

"That's why I'm here," he said.

"Will you hand over your device?" she asked.

"I'm not the bad guy, you know," he said defensively.

"But you are the heavy guy!" I complained. "Ouch—move your elbow, Saunders—I can't breathe!"

Albert sent a memo that said **SPLAT**, along with a

strangled feeling. His arms wriggled below Saunders's big knees.

Hastily, Saunders opened the door and got out, but he immediately slipped on some ice. Just that quick he went down and was planted in the snow with his legs in a pretzel. I met his eyes from the open door. "You don't look like a secret agent."

"And what does a secret agent look like, Miss Day?" Saunders got back up with a very grumpy expression.

"I don't know. Like Double-O-Seven, I guess. Not like Double-O-Butt-in-the-Snow."

Saunders brushed the snow from his dark jacket and slacks. "Ha ha," he said, sounding very un-agent-like. Brit and Lars chuckled quietly.

"So, Saunders, was Brit right in thinking that you guys were going to haul us off for questioning?" I asked.

"Brit is sharp," Saunders said with a nod.

"Then why aren't you busting us right now?" Lars asked.

"Even in my line of work, this is unusual. It's more than unusual. And I didn't exactly agree when my boss gave the order to—anyway, I want more information."

Brit eyed him shrewdly. "And you'd get more information by tagging along with us—right?"

"Right again, Brit. You should come to work for us."

Brit frowned. "I don't think I'd like working for the military industrial establishment."

I had to smile.

Saunders made a sound like he was tired. "Sometimes I don't like it either," he said with a scowl. I figured he was thinking about the lie he'd told, about taking us to find Ma when really he had orders to lock us up. But he quickly shook off his guilt. "So where's your Uncle Commodore?" he asked with a hint of sarcasm.

I scanned the parking lot. A snowplow had scraped out about six parking places, piling the snow in a truck-size mound. The one street light that serviced the lot was glowing cheerfully, as was the Steak Night activity sign. But the three SMHR units were nowhere to be seen.

"Maybe they went inside," I said, "to appear less conspicuous."

Brit made a skeptical face. "It's sort of hard for those three to be inconspicuous."

Unexpectedly, Agent Saunders handed Brit his communication device. "Here, take it. I'm on your side. I want you kids to trust me."

Brit took it. "The jury is still out," she said coldly. She listened briefly to the earpiece and gave it a shake. "Hello, Commodore?" There was no response. "Well, let's go check inside."

We walked up the wheelchair ramp and opened the big door. I was hit with a blast of warmth and delicious aromas. "*Mmm*, something smells good." The clock on the wall said seven-o-five. I realized I'd only gotten one piece of pizza, and I was starving again.

The barnlike community room was a sea of tables and chairs, but there were only four or five people eating. In the corner was the big-screen TV, droning on about the news of the snowstorm.

There was a noisy clinking and clanking coming from the kitchen, and the cooks emerged from a swinging door. They were wearing the "Adeline Seniors Rock" aprons that were popular in our town. The aprons had black silhouettes of rocking chairs above generous patchwork pockets. Laden with pans and platters of food, the cooks marched deliberately toward us, strangely choreographed tall to short, moving in robot lockstep.

It was our missing SMHR units looking weirder than ever.

They set the pans and platters down on a table by the emergency exit. There was a beautiful potato dish, a lush salad, and a three layer chocolate cake.

Mr. Noguchi, the regular cook, was peering from the kitchen service window with his hands on his hips and a very puzzled expression on his face.

The Commodore gestured to the little feast on the table. "We have mastered the culinary arts," he announced.

29
Debrief

It seemed a little odd to me that the SMHR units were helping us like this. Not only did they distract Agent Saunders so that we could get out of the house, but they'd even lent us their car to escape. And now they had bothered to cook us supper?

"Why are you SMHR units doing all this?" I asked. "Aren't you just supposed to be gathering data?"

My question seemed to baffle them for a moment. They all blinked as one, and then Citizen Lady said, "Indeed; gathering data is what we do. However, when the home-plane anticipated danger and damage and, thus, urged the triad's prompt return, we concluded this action countered our commitment to data acquisition."

Her longwinded reply didn't really answer my question, so I tried again. "But why are you helping *us*?"

"*Helping* is useful for accumulating data, and this triad chose to be useful."

This still sounded like double-talk to me.

Med Tech Tek got more to the point. "To do otherwise was stressful. We chose to reduce the vexing anxiety by ignoring protocol and helping. It was the obvious solution."

"I guess that makes sense. But you guys cooked us supper; that was nice and very thoughtful."

"We were correctly reminded by Med Tech Tek that you humans might need a protein and carbohydrate break," the Commodore said, "especially after all of the taxing activity. And choosing the Center of Seniors seemed an excellent rendezvous point for easy access to food, as well as a low probability of discovery—perhaps you have noticed that many seniors are afflicted with poor eyesight and diminished hearing?"

"You've got a point, Mr. Commodore," I said. "This all looks really good." I felt almost faint with hunger. I ran and got a plate and some cutlery from the service window. Lars followed, and Brit and Albert were right behind. We all sat down and served ourselves and for once Albert didn't pick at his food. He ate with a concentration that he usually reserved for counting dust.

"I could not burn the bovine," Citizen Lady said sadly, "despite the proclamation of Steak Night and 1-Buck Bingo. But I discovered nuts and cheese and yams . . . they should offer sufficient caloric sustenance."

"And here," said Med Tech Tek, "we have *cake*, which

is nearly void of nutrition, but very attractive. You'll note that I applied the frosting as instructions dictated, and then added my own design with the geometric swirl in the crème product." Med Tech Tek had created an amazing design of white tree limb-fractals on top of chocolate frosting. It was the most beautiful cake I'd ever seen.

"You are an artist, Med Tech Tek! And you did an awesome job with everyone's new eyes."

His face and smile clearly showed pleasure. "Thank you very much for the compliment, Pearl."

"Pearl?" Agent Saunders asked.

"It's just a nickname," I said.

"While you take in the calories, we need to formulate a strategy," the Commodore urged. "Agent Saunders, your skill set may be helpful, so pay attention."

Agent Saunders looked annoyed. "I always pay attention," he muttered. "That *is* my skill set."

"We need to debrief," the Commodore said briskly, oblivious to the fact that he had just insulted the agent. "At this juncture, the negative energies continue to leak from the half-constant, and with each physical disturbance of the site, the flow increases. The negative thoughts seem to be attracted to any and all beings who are conscious— particularly to that which is conscious and positive. The negative energy works quickly to overwhelm the positive, and then all these thoughts bleed back to the half-constant where the negative pressure is already too great. Alas, it becomes—what is the term?—a vicious cycle."

"So where does Albert come into the picture?" I asked. I tasted the cake and it melted in my mouth like a chocolaty brownie dipped in whipped cream.

The Commodore's turquoise eyes sparkled. "The triad proposes that—" all of a sudden, an ear-splitting blast of feedback squawked from Brit's jacket pocket. *SCHREE-AUCH!* Brit jumped at the sound. It was the communication device. She retrieved it from her pocket and set it on the table; it emitted a high-pitched cackle. "Watch the TV, Saunders!"

It was the crazy Partner again.

"I'm going to blast that alien cloud." He began to laugh hysterically, sounding totally off his rocker. There were gunshots. He wasn't using the silencer anymore. "Oops! Got one of ours. Sorry, buddy-boy."

At that moment, the big TV in the corner flashed to "BREAKING NEWS." It was the eye-in-the-sky chopper reporter for Channel Seven, and she was panning her camera to show a view of *my street!* It was swarming with the BETI guys—I recognized their hazmat suits. But the announcer claimed they were police officers and that the house in question was a meth lab. The camera panned down on the roof of poor Mr. Shinn's house. Then, to the surprise

of the news reporter, there was a flash of red in the woods—
and it coincided with the gunshots the Partner was firing
that we all heard from the earpiece! The scarlet flair turned
into an explosion, blasting straight up. It looked eerily like
a mushroom cloud, only thinner and redder. The spotlights
from the BETI ground-crew gave it a hellish glow.

"Oh my God, what has he done?" Brit gasped.

30
This is not a drill

Saunders was on his cell phone. "Yes, ma'am, it's me. You've got to stand down and get the team out of there. I took a ride in the AV and they are the real deal. No, they claim it's interdimensional. No! Everything you throw at it will only make it worse. Then get clearance from higher up. I said—"

At that moment, a siren blared. It was right outside and loud enough to rattle the overhead lights. The siren paused. "THIS IS NOT A DRILL," a lady's voice said calmly, and then the siren resumed.

"What is *that*?" Saunders yelled.

"It sounds like the siren for the dam!" Brit shouted.

"What dam?" Sanders demanded.

"The earth dam above Adeline," she shouted back. "They test it every Wednesday for evacuation. But they test it at noon—never at nighttime. I can't believe the dam would burst. Not now, when the ground is frozen."

"It didn't burst," Saunders hollered, shaking his head. "This is classic BETI. They're going to get everyone out for their safety *and* for national security. This dam business is just an excuse. What's the normal procedure here?"

"Everyone is supposed to head up the hill to the church." The noise of the siren was hurting my head.

"THIS IS NOT A DRILL." The voice of the calm lady echoed over the loudspeaker—and the siren wailed on.

"They'll bus the entire population out of town," Saunders said decisively. "It'll be a total evacuation, probably a thirty-mile perimeter. Your mom and grandmother should be safe for now."

"This noise is vexing," the Commodore said loudly. He almost sounded irritated. "We need quiet to discuss strategy. Where does Mrs. Rona Zucker dwell?"

"About two blocks from here," I shouted. "Why?"

The Commodore and the other two SMHR units got up from the table and started heading for the exit. "We shall borrow the Zucker dwelling for a second rendezvous," said the Commodore.

I got up and grabbed a piece of cake for the road. So did Lars. "Mr. Commodore, to get to the Zuckers you need to go left on Dibble and right on Rock. She's the third house down—the one with the gnomes and fake deer in the yard!"

"We'll drive—you walk," he said flatly. The three

SMHRs were out of there and the door was closing behind them.

"THIS IS NOT A DRILL."

Brit and Lars were putting on their coats while I rushed to get Albert all zipped up. By the time we got outside, the SMHRs and the V-dub were gone. The loudspeaker on the light pole was wailing at ear-popping decibels, so we got away from there as fast as we could. People were beginning to fill the streets. We were going against the crowd that was bustling in the opposite direction, up the big hill to Saint Aloysius.

As we hurried along, I said, "Keep your eyes out for Ma and Meemaw and Mrs. Zucker. If they see us, they'll just worry and we don't have time to explain all this crazy stuff."

We tried to keep our collars up and our heads down so we wouldn't be recognized. I noticed that the townspeople were not panicking. They were walking with brisk and serious attitudes, but there was no running or pushing. People were corralling the little kids and walking patiently with the elderly. Just bunches of folks keeping their eyes on each other, puffing out little worried clouds in the cold night air. I liked my town at that moment.

"You kids need to go the other way." It was Mr. Kahn, who owned the blueberry farm.

"We will," I assured him. "We just need to meet up with some—some people."

We took a shortcut down an alley and peeked over a fence to watch Mrs. Zucker's house. Ma and Meemaw and Mrs. Zucker were leaving, carefully stepping down the porch stairs, bundled up like they were going to the Arctic. They carried what looked like bags of groceries. *Be prepared* was Meemaw's policy. As soon as they were out of sight, we ran to the house. I was surprised to see the front door fling open—I was afraid we'd been caught, but it was just Med Tech Tek. The SMHR units were already inside.

Citizen Lady and the Commodore were clearing the table in the dining room. It was littered with the remnants of the meatloaf dinner that Mrs. Zucker and Ma and Meemaw had been eating not fifteen minutes before.

"How'd you get here so fast?" I asked.

"That would require a technical explanation," the Commodore said shortly. He still seemed a little irritated. We could hear the alarm droning, but it wasn't nearly as loud as it had been at the Senior Center.

"Come sit down," Citizen Lady urged.

Mrs. Zucker's house was overly warm and crammed with furniture, books, and dusty knickknacks. Her piano top was crowded with pictures of her grandchildren. A big one in the center featured her husband, Vintner, who had died a few years earlier. He had been an ugly man with kind eyes. It made me think it was good that Ma and Meemaw had been here tonight. It would have been pretty scary for old Mrs. Zucker to get evacuated by herself. It could be hard for old folks to be by themselves. I guessed I would never have that problem as long as Albert was around.

"So, what were you going to propose?" Brit asked, facing the Commodore.

"Lure it all back," the Commodore said with a deliberate head-bob. "The triad theorizes that the negative energies will be drawn to an amplified positive charge. So if Albert can initiate a new channel-opening and bait that space with positive energies, and if our integral craft can amplify that charge, then perhaps we can *trick* the poison back to the source."

Albert nodded, agreeing with the precept of this strategy.

"That doesn't sound too bad," I said. "Albert can just put his hand on the panel back in your lab and—" I realized the SMHRs were frowning and wagging their heads. I didn't like the way they were looking at me. "What?" I demanded.

31
Bleak

I t is imperative that Albert work from your father's laboratory," Citizen Lady said in a firm and unyielding tone.

"Why? You guys have way better machinery."

"Because a new opening requires the use of lasers to soften the dimensional membrane. Albert can't facilitate a channel without them. Our machinery has its limits. It is configured for SMHR units, not humans—and the lasers are already in place. The garage is equipped with everything you need." Citizen Lady said this like it was the final word.

"Why don't *you* do it? You know how."

"The triad knows how but we cannot make it work. As the Commodore explained before, this task requires consciousness, not computation." Citizen Lady seemed a smidge bummed out about this fact.

"Couldn't Albert leave some bait around the existing tear in the woods?"

"Impossible," the Commodore said. "That channel is emitting too strong a negative stream. It cannot be reversed. Albert must construct a new channel for the bait."

"Why didn't we do this on Mars, where it was safe?" Lars asked.

"Equations predicted that this strategy would not work at such a distance," Med Tech Tek replied. "It must be on Earth, and it is only logical to utilize the system already in place."

"I don't see how Albert is supposed to throw enough happiness at a new opening to trick the bad thoughts into following—especially if he has to work in the garage, which is way too close to the red mist." I shook my head. "I really don't like the sound of this plan."

"That is why he will need his counterparts. He will require support from all of you." Citizen Lady sounded a little sad, but she was very firm. "I am confident that I can adjust our energy amplifier to enhance whatever positive thoughts he provides."

Lars looked grim. "This idea sucks. But I don't know what else we can do."

"Success is unlikely," the Commodore agreed.

"Well you're encouraging," Brit said sourly.

"I recognize sarcasm," the Commodore stated. "Success is still unlikely."

"Do you realize that if the bad energy spreads, there

will be war and chaos everywhere?" Brit shuddered. "People would be their angriest, most paranoid selves, like crazy Mr. Shinn and Mrs. Wagner and the Partner . . . " Brit glanced at Saunders and her eyes looked sorry.

"Even the poor animals," I added. "It just makes me sick to think about it. It'll be a horrible world."

"I can assure you that such a thing will not happen," Med Tech Tek said.

"You mean the mist won't spread like that?" Brit asked.

"I mean the imbalance will be righted when the universe is sucked inside out and annihilated. This will occur before all are infected."

We stared at Med Tech Tek.

Albert sent me a memo with a dark cloud that said **Bleak**.

"This just gets worse and worse," Brit said heatedly. "I didn't think it would happen so fast."

She must have understood this was a possibility when she watched the movie back on the SMHR craft—that sickening one where the numbers got sucked through the ring.

"Med Tech, are you sure about this inside out business?" Agent Saunders asked.

"My calculations are accurate, I am sorry to say."

Gloom hung heavy over the dining room table. Finally, I said, "In a way, it frees us."

"What do you mean, it frees us?" Brit asked.

"There is no *what if* to this situation. I mean, we're dead ducks, so we might as well be super bold because we have nothing to lose."

"Mary's right," Lars said. His expression became determined and a little amused. "We might as well be super bold."

"Hold on—" My phone was buzzing in my pocket. "Hi, Ma?" I went to the front room to talk.

"Mary, thank goodness I got through. This is just crazy, but they're evacuating Adeline!"

"What? Why?" I was trying to sound really surprised. Plus I hoped Ma hadn't seen our road on the news. It would be one more thing for her to worry about, and what good would that do?

"The siren for the dam went off," Ma continued. "I don't know if it's legit or not, but they're playing it safe. We're up at the church and so is most of the town!"

"THIS IS NOT A DRILL," the tireless lady said in the background.

"I wish they'd turn that damn thing off!" It was Meemaw, complaining nearby.

"I'm sorry we didn't bring snacks for you and Brit," Ma said. "You could make milkshakes; there's a little ice cream."

"It's okay, Ma. We made pizza."

"I wish I were home," Ma said longingly. "Is Albert okay?"

"We're fine. We're out of the valley so no flood here." I hated lying to Ma.

"I know. Well, I imagine we'll just hang out at the church for a few hours. Either a sensor is wacky up on the dam or we'll see water in the street. What a dumb day!"

"I kind of miss you," I said.

"I kind of miss you, too. Brit's staying over, right?"

"Yeah, she's here. Plus Lars is going to hang out with us for a while. We were going to watch a show or something."

"Tell Lars thank you."

"Ma says thank you Lars."

He nodded.

"Honey, are you okay?"

Ma heard something in my sad pause.

"I was just thinking that I love you."

"I love you, too, Mary. Tell Albert good night, and Happy New Year."

"Good night, Ma. Happy New Year to you, too."

My eyes rested on Albert sitting at the table. He appeared to be oblivious, staring at the piano, but I knew he was thinking. He was always thinking. "Ma says Happy New Year, Albert."

He memoed me the smiley pearl.

The Commodore was still talking strategy and calculations.

I looked down at my phone and felt a bittersweet twinge of missing Ma and Meemaw, but also a huge sense of gratitude that Albert was here with me. I realized that since Ma first brought Albert home from the hospital, he had sent me a memo every single day showing me that I was a girl like a pearl, like the most special in all the world. His memos had helped me be positive and confident and happy. Albert might have been sort of weird but he was the best brother I coulda gotten.

It was too bad the whole world couldn't get a nice memo. With all this rotten stuff going on and being on the brink of disaster, it seemed like that's what everybody needed—a giant memo to remind us of everything good in our lives. There must have been tons of good stuff out there; like enough positive energy to—

Something like a light bulb went on in my head.

"Hey, Mr. Commodore, I have an idea."

Everyone at the table turned to look at me. "Contribute," he said, sounding a lot like a robot—which I guess was what he was, sort of.

"You guys are good at communication, right? I mean you collect and transmit data, like that's your job, right?"

"Indeed."

"I've been thinking about strategy. It seems that tricking the bad thoughts to go back to the half-constant only solves half of the problem. There's still that imbalance that's forcing stuff out, and the imbalance has to be fixed or we have that vicious cycle, like the Commodore said."

"I concur," said Med Tech Tek. The other two SMHR units nodded in agreement.

"So maybe we could make a happy commercial. People do it all the time. They make things seem fantastic with good pictures and a bit of nice music. I remember this commercial about coffee that would always get Ma all teary-eyed, and it was just coffee! Anyhow, that's my idea." I watched to see their reaction. I wasn't sure I was on the right track because I was thinking that surely one of them would have thought of this.

Brit got it right away. "It might work," she said. "Like a message to get people to think positive thoughts."

Lars stared at his sister and then he got it, too. "According to you SMHR units, all thoughts flow to the half-constant, and if they're good ones, maybe the balance could be restored that way."

"That should ease the pressure," Saunders added, "which, according to the visitors, is what's forcing the stuff into our dimension in the first place."

"That's right." I nodded enthusiastically. "And then maybe the rip would naturally seal, the way you guys described it."

"That is an interesting proposal." The Commodore bobbed his head and his turquoise eyes sparkled. "A marketing strategy to elicit positive energies—this could be very useful." He and his comrades nodded as one.

Albert sent me two smiley pearls and for a split second he looked into my eyes.

"What are we waiting for?" said Brit. "Let's *go*."

32
Super bold

The SMHR units had left the Volkswagen idling in Rona's carport. It mostly looked like a normal V-Dub but it kept doing a jumpy, shimmer thing, and that didn't look normal at all.

Once again we all squeezed into the snug interior. Up in the front seat, the SMHR units sat quietly. The Commodore was driving, concentrating on whatever it was he concentrated on. In the back seat, Albert was sitting on my lap and Brit was sitting on Lars's lap. Agent Saunders was squished in between us. Talk about sardines in a can.

When we started off, the billowing cloud accompanied us, but once we were up, the Commodore eased off on the fog and we were able to see the view. The moon peeked out from behind a cloud, shining on the scene below.

There was a parade of busses making their way south on 266. They were going in the opposite direction of us; Ma and

Meemaw were getting farther and farther away from home. It sort of made my heart hurt to think of it. As I watched, one bus skidded to a stop and people poured out the door, shoving and fighting. All those nice people who had been helping each other in Adeline were now on the road, yelling and punching and being awful. If only they knew they were being poisoned by something that didn't belong here. I just hoped Ma wasn't on that bus.

"I bet Ma is trying to call me right now. Can we get calls up here?" I asked.

"Not in flight," Med Tech Tek said. "Our electronics interfere with your devices."

I sighed.

It seemed like the Commodore was driving slower than he normally did. I was glad because it gave me time to think. Below us, the lights of Adeline twinkled. They grew small as we crossed the valley, past fields where snow banished fences and borders. Everything looked so soft and pretty in the light of the moon that I wanted to hold on to the moment. I closed my eyes.

In summertime there were strawberries down there, and over the bridge was Kahn's U-pick Blueberry Farm. In the fall, Zucker's Corn Maze—run by Rona's brother-in-law, Earl—did a steady business with schoolchildren and families in search of activities in the country. It was really lame, that dumb corn maze, but the little kids loved it. We went there in second grade and learned about corn, and Brit threw up on the bus on the way back to school. I noticed that Brit was watching the scenery, too. Then all of a sudden we were looking at each other. Her eyes were glassy with tears, and so were mine.

I reached over and held Brit's hand. We knew we were heading into terrible danger; it was like we were going to war.

"Zucker's Corn Maze," I said with a sad smile.

"I hurled on the bus." She grinned.

"It was so gross."

We started to laugh.

Lars reached out his lanky hand and gripped both of our hands. And then Albert pointed his finger and barely tapped the top of Lars's hand—he didn't usually do that sort of thing. With his little finger-tap, I got a memo loud and clear, like a trumpet blast. It said **SUPER BOLD**.

The SMHR-vehicle was back in the cloud. The Commodore must have turned on the fog machine.

"After you disembark, the triad will transmit the commercial," Citizen Lady said.

"Wait, what are you going to say?" I asked.

Without fanfare, Citizen Lady recited, "People of Earth,

it is critical at this juncture that you facilitate profound happiness." She seemed satisfied with her marketing sound-bite.

Brit and I shared faces of extreme disapproval.

I imagined Citizen Lady broadcasting her message. She would sound about as warm and fuzzy as the annoying THIS IS NOT A DRILL voice. I tried to be polite. "Citizen Lady, I'm thinking that maybe one of *us* should do the talking. I think it would be more sincere coming from—you know—a human being."

The SMHR units considered this for about two seconds. "Agreed," they all said.

"It should be Mary." Brit squeezed my hand. "Mary's good at making people feel better."

"That's true," Lars interjected. "She just did it a few minutes ago."

Albert memoed me a silly thumbs-up.

I felt a growing panic when it began to dawn on me that I'd have to say something to tons of people. I didn't like being the center of attention. What was the right thing to say? What were the words? Getting wedged into making this commercial was starting to make me feel sick—but then I remembered *super bold* and I considered the alternative; annihilation was definitely worse than stage fright. Yeah, I could do this.

Med Tech Tek turned to Saunders. "As soon as you are able, call your superiors to reiterate that they *must* stay away from the anomaly."

Saunders nodded.

"We'll unlock the garage door remotely," the Commodore said. "And once the lasers are engaged, we should be able to recalibrate them to cut a new channel next to the old one. Albert's job is to power up the machine and mentally construct the fractals into their proper algorithms."

"What about the commercial?" I asked. "How are you guys going to film it and broadcast it?"

"Easily accomplished from our—er, automobile," Med Tech Tek said. "The triad will signal the lab and our integral craft can transmit the message far and wide."

"Okay. Okay," I repeated nervously. "I just gotta think of what to say."

"The timing will be tricky," Citizen Lady said gravely. "As soon as Pearl attempts inspirational thought, the negative energies will swarm to overwhelm her. It is critical that the channel is baited and operational before Pearl speaks. The energies *must* be distracted."

"So Mary has to fight off all the negative energy and give a speech to the entire world at the same time? No pressure there," Brit said sarcastically.

33
Remember my love

The V-dub had stopped buzzing. "We have arrived," Citizen Lady said.

Albert opened the door and got off my lap. I followed Albert, and then Agent Saunders wriggled out, unfolding himself like someone emerging from a clown car.

Once he was out, Saunders immediately called his boss and told her to keep the BETI force away and to keep the local police and press away, too. Hopefully they had enough clout to make this happen. I fought the urge to call Ma and Meemaw. If they weren't acting like themselves, I was afraid I couldn't do what I had to do—no, I couldn't call them.

"Pearl will commence the commercial as soon as the triad detects a backward flow of energy," the Commodore stated. "At that point we will give a signal."

"Wait, what's the signal?"

At that, the car lit up like a lamp. It glowed softly pink, illuminating the snow and the billowing fog.

"Pink light—got it." I bobbed my head, trying to look attentive. "And how are you going to amplify Albert's thoughts?"

"As soon as we measure a sufficient charge, we can amplify it exponentially right at the mouth of the new channel." This time a thin blue beam shot out of the left headlight.

"Okay, the blue beam is the amplifier." I stood there for a long moment. Brit and Lars came and stood by me and Albert. We had stuff to do, but I was reluctant to see the triad go. "Well, thank you for everything, guys." I smiled at the three oddball SMHR units, squished in the front of their ridiculous flying Volkswagen. Maybe they were just machines, but they had gone above and beyond their jobs. They were funny individuals, and they made the choice to help us. That seemed pretty nice to me.

"Mr. Commodore, Citizen Lady, Med Tech Tek, I believe you are way more than just data collectors."

The Commodore's turquoise eyes glistened. "Thank you," he acknowledged, and he showed me one last crazy smile.

I held up my hand and waved their silly four-fingered wave. "Goodbye."

The three SMHR units did the same. Then the doors of the Bug closed with a click, and the vehicle hummed and pulsated. We stood back as it lit up like a welding torch. The buzz it emitted tickled my temples and ran down my spine. The now-familiar fog puffed and billowed as the car assumed the shape of a flying saucer, which rose in the air. It disappeared behind the cloud it created, but I had to assume it was up there, hovering, ready to play its part.

The fog followed the Bug, clearing the air where we stood. I was amazed to see we were in the middle of our backyard. I didn't notice any BETI guys; hopefully they had all retreated. The scratchy, unnerving feeling of the red mist was strong, but it wasn't as bad as it could have been. For some reason, most of the energy was shooting straight up like a geyser, but it had to be going somewhere—and somewhere it was seeking conscious minds to ruin.

Albert sent me a memo that described the mental trick that helped keep the spiders from settling in. He accompanied it with a cartoon of three people—Saunders and Lars and Brit—with ice cubes on top of their heads. **Protection essential,** he memoed.

"Albert says you've got to know how to keep the red mist out of your heads."

The three of them paid close attention as I tried to explain. "The trick is to imagine your mind is a snowy landscape and it's all clean and white and cold. It's like you build an icy wall around the field that is your mind—but you *have* to stay calm. I think this makes it too boring for the red spiders to be drawn in. It worked for me, for a while. Just be as neutral and boring as you can."

"Like Saunders." Brit smirked.

"Hilarious," he replied.

I ignored their sparring. "Lars, is your guitar in the truck?"

"Yeah, why?"

"I think we could use some music for the commercial. You know, for the mood."

"I'll go get it," he agreed.

Saunders pushed his hat down in a determined way. "What was it you said back there, Mary—that we might as well be super bold?" He grinned a tight half-smile. "Operation Super Bold in progress."

When we reached the garage, we discovered that the SMHR units didn't exactly open the lock—they blasted it to smithereens. Saunders pushed the door and we all filed in.

"Albert, you get started," Saunders said as he flipped on the lights. "I'm going to stand guard outside."

"Hey, Saunders—" Brit tossed him the earpiece. "Thanks for not turning us in. You're okay."

"Copy that," he replied, all business except for a slight upward twitch of his mouth.

Albert memoed me a picture of the electrode thingies. They had to get placed on his head with some kind of gel—he promptly handed me a tube of the stuff.

"Brit, help me. We have to stick these on Albert's scalp."

Brit and I hurriedly placed the electrodes while Albert fiddled with the machinery.

"Mary, what are you going to say?" Brit asked.

"I'm not sure. The only stuff I know about is you guys and living here on Myrtle Road."

As I placed the electrodes on Albert, I kept thinking about my life. It was a small life with Ma and Meemaw and Albert and good old Brit. We didn't do big things or go on neat vacations. The grades I got at school were just okay. But I had to admit I liked my life. Ma loved us, and so did Meemaw in her blustery way. And I had a best friend who I could depend on and laugh with—it only took one arch of an eyebrow. Brit had Lars, and I had Albie. And that's all I knew for sure on this New Year's Eve.

Lars showed up at the door with his guitar in hand. He'd run from the truck and was breathing hard, making little clouds in the cold garage. He put the guitar strap over his head. "Ready when you are."

"I guess I'll be ready when Albert is."

Albert sat on a tall stool, his head a tangle of wires, like a little Medusa. He'd already powered up the computer. For a moment he was stymied by a demand for a password. Finally he typed *remembermylove* and he was in. He flipped the toggle switch and then muscled the big lever to ON. From the window came a white flash accompanied by an electrical sound—like clashing light sabers. Hopefully the lasers had engaged. Albert conferred this was so by showing me six white lines, like the spokes of a wheel, converging at a white-hot center. I guessed that was how the lasers "softened" the dimensional membrane.

Next he was prompted on-screen for an equation, which he entered, and things began to happen on their own. His face went blank as he concentrated inward, conjuring his thought puzzles, constructing the fractals smaller and smaller to tunnel into the half-constant.

Albert stared and stared at the screen, trying to find his way. His pupils were black manholes and his baby face was tense. *Good, brave Albie*, I thought—but as I did, the spiders swarmed around me. I couldn't linger long on sentimental thoughts. Remember the icy wall, the snowy blank slate. Stay calm.

Suddenly Albert memoed **I-AM-IN.**

34
The commercial

Albert shared a tree-limb pattern that repeated and repeated until it was a tunnel that twisted like a white wormhole in a vast darkness. He sent thoughts of joy into the wormhole—little things that pleased him; like math, and Ma, and natural beauty, and Pearl.

"You're doing a really good job, Albie," I said quietly. I wanted to support him but not distract him. I wished the blue beam would kick in to amplify the bait. But even without the amplifier there came a subtle vibration and a change in the atmosphere.

"Do you feel that?" Brit asked. "Something is happening."

When I looked out the window I could see the white light of the lasers flashing in the heart of the red mist, but the red stuff had stopped spewing from the rip, and now it just hovered. Slowly, slowly the mist began to reverse itself. It rolled in sluggish waves back toward the six posts. The woods seemed to blur with the sickening crawl of it, and I felt a little carsick watching.

Why weren't the SMHRs using the amplifier? The mist was traveling backward—but very slowly.

We were startled when the little TV in the corner turned on; the triad must have done it remotely. The local news was showing one bad thing after another. Animals were acting crazy, just like poor Beau. People were lashing out for the dumbest reasons, starting fights with friends and family. There were altercations in restaurants and on trains because the other guy looked different—or for no reason at all. One messed-up boy shot his best friend and there were dozens of road-rage incidents. The red spiders were doing their worst; the infection had begun. "Oh, Brit!" I could feel the yucky energy scuttling around me but a wave of self-loathing reminded me to stay calm. I fashioned the icy wall and imagined the frozen wasteland. Calm and boring, I tried to tell myself.

"This is gross," Brit said. "Why would the Commodore want us to watch it?" She switched the channel and found a shot of Times Square, where the New Year's throng had gathered to celebrate. But things were getting out of hand there, too; several fights had broken out and the crowd seemed agitated.

Suddenly the pink light was shining outside. Hopefully

Albert could keep sending the bait of good energy. The bad stuff *had* to be distracted while I gave my speech.

"It's the signal! Come on, Lars, let's go. Brit, would you stay with Albie? I'll leave the door open."

Lars and I tromped out into the snow. I could see Agent Saunders standing very still over by the compost. "You okay, Saunders?"

He gave me a sober thumbs-up. "Good luck, kid."

"Hey Lars, what's that tune they always play on New Year's—'Old Sing-Sang'?"

"It's called 'Auld Lang Syne,'" he corrected. "It's a song about the good old days."

"Can you play it?"

"I can figure it out."

"Try playing it really slow, and sort of sad."

He nodded and began to search for the notes. It didn't take him long before he could play the tune, and he played it amazingly well.

With Lars plinking "Auld Lang Syne" on the guitar, and with the pale, pink light shining, I gathered myself to speak.

"Okay." I coughed once. "Lars, do you feel the spiders?"

"No. They're still distracted." He gave me the thumbs-up.

I was wasting time. I just had to dive in.

"Happy New Year, Earth," I said in a serious voice. "Where I live it's snowy and it's as pretty as it can be. Maybe in your town there's snow on the ground, or maybe it's raining and the air is getting all cleaned up. Maybe it's warm and there's a nice, balmy breeze. It could be night or it could be day, but here on Earth, it's home."

"Mary, you're on TV!" Brit shouted from inside the garage.

I could see her pointing at the little TV while Albert concentrated, not moving a muscle. *Good boy*, I thought. But *I* had to concentrate, too. How could I possibly say the right thing—who did I think I was?

Sister and daughter and friend. Good and nice. The positive memo appeared with a warm glow that felt like home. Albert was doing his job and still looking out for me. I shifted my feet and looked down at my hands. I was startled to see the ten different colors of polish on my nails. I thought of Brit and me and the dorky fun we had and of other kids who just wanted to be kids. My colorful nails made me feel a lot better. I checked with Lars and he nodded. I could do this. I had to do this.

I cleared my throat and continued. "At my house I have my Ma and my Meemaw, and my little brother. Ma is a hard worker and she takes life as it comes. Mostly she sees the good in people, and she doesn't judge—well, except for my dad, who died. I think she's mad at him because he left her alone. But she's not really alone. She's got lots of love around her.

"My Meemaw is a bit prickly but she's willing to learn new lessons even though she's older. She's got our backs and we love her for that—for being strong and fierce.

"My best friend who I go to school with is so loyal and smart, and she's good to me, even though she's way smarter than I am. But she is never a know-it-all and she believes in me. So I love her lots.

"Her big brother is playing the guitar right now, and he is so good that the song is almost breaking my heart. He's secretly really smart even though he hides it to be tough and strong, and he's good at car engines and the guitar and I wish he were my big brother because he's so awesome."

Lars was delicately picking the tune—*for auld lang syne, my dear, for auld lang syne*—

"My own brother is like the smartest, most unique-est kid in the whole world. All my life since he was born, he's been sharing his good and beautiful thoughts with me. He made me what I am today—which is happy. And that's why I'm talking to you right now, to remind you of the happiness of small things—"

Albert interrupted my dialogue with an urgent memo. **One laser is offline.** With that, the pink light turned off and I was standing alone in the darkness.

35
Going to war

Laser Offline! he memoed again. An image appeared in my head of a disengaged wire and a red exclamation mark that kept jumping. Albert followed it up with a picture of one of the six posts—the one that was closest to the trail. **Easy fix—black tape!!** I noticed that inside the garage Albert was holding a spool of tape. He waggled it to get me moving.

"Oh, great," I said to Lars. "There's a messed-up wire in the woods. I gotta go fix it!"

"Where is it?" Lars asked.

"On the post nearest the trail." I darted into the garage and snatched the tape from Albert. He reminded me to keep cold and calm by placing the image of a frozen pond in my mind's eye. I nodded at him and then I hurried back out.

At the doorway, Lars grabbed the tape from me. "I'll do it," he said like there was no argument. "I'm good at fixing things."

"Lars, don't go," Brit begged him from the door—but he was already running down the trail.

"Keep the snow in your mind!" Brit yelled after him.

Albert had to turn the big lever to OFF so that Lars could make the repair. The screeching sound of the lasers stopped and the white light immediately vanished. Now the red spiders grew restless; they had no bait to chase. They probed and scuttled with mean little thoughts. Be calm, I told myself, be icy calm. "Brit, we can't be fearful right now."

"It should have been you," she said bitterly. "Albert could have protected you with his memos. There's no one out there to protect Lars." Her eyes had gone shifty and mean.

"Brit, please don't give in to the anger. Remember the icy wall."

"Right," she whispered. "You're right." Her face was as pale as the snow she envisioned.

I realized that the TV was on and there was a girl talking.

"They've been playing a loop of it, over and over," Brit said. "You're on that big sign above Times Square."

The sweet notes from Lars's guitar sang in the background, and there I was, standing in the snow in a dark forest with the pink light shining down. I looked small and determined. In a voice that was like melancholy music, I talked about my family and Brit and Lars. But this Mary didn't exactly look like me—and she didn't exactly *sound* like me, either. She could have been anyone's daughter, talking about anyone's family.

The crowd was silent as they watched me on the high-up electronic billboard, waiting, wondering what this was about. I don't know how *they* felt, but here in the garage I was glad to have this reminder of small things that are big. As I spoke in Times Square, *BREAKING NEWS* showed a segment in the corner that flipped to channels all over the world, and to websites, too. In all those places I spoke all their languages! There I was on the news in Italy, and Russia, and Nigeria, and South Korea . . . the Commodore had put our commercial all over the globe.

I remembered with a start that I had to stay neutral! The evil thoughts were sneaking in and my distrust of those people watching in Times Square and the people watching in those other countries had become my main concern. I froze the angry thoughts in midair and I raised the icy wall just in time.

Suddenly Albert memoed **Laser back online,** and he reached to flip the large lever to ON. Once again the white light flashed in the forest. The electrical sound buzzed and screeched. Albert intently watched the screen.

"Lars must have fixed it," Brit said hopefully. She waited by the door, biting a nail.

Across the room Albert sat rigidly on his tall stool,

focusing inward, creating the fractals to open the wormhole again. He was getting better at it—it wasn't long before he memoed the image of the tunnel that twisted and writhed as he filled it with his best thoughts.

"There's Lars," Brit announced. She was smiling expectantly, the relief shining in her eyes. "Thank goodness you're back!" she hailed—but it was an angry Lars that pushed past her and he lunged at me, smacking me hard in the face. He was flushed and fidgety and his eyes were horribly bloodshot. He raised his fist to pound me again, but there was Agent Saunders in the doorway. Just that quick, Saunders chopped a secret agent move on Lars's neck.

Poor Lars collapsed, and Saunders set him gently on the concrete floor.

"Sorry about that, kid," Saunders said in a husky voice.

The smack I'd taken from Lars kicked in and I saw stars. I staggered, but Brit held my arm to steady me.

Albert stayed on task, still sending the good energy as best he could, but a noise had begun outside—or maybe it was inside my mind. It was like a howling monster scraping on metal. The red mist stalled and hovered. It lay frozen in the air, as if undecided about which way to go. And then it chose a direction. Lazy waves of red began to roll through the forest away from the rip, heading back out into the world where it could find billions of conscious minds to ruin.

Albert memoed a message of **DANGER** that felt stressed and brittle and ready to snap. My head was throbbing from where Lars hit me, and a gnawing fear was growing in my gut. "Icy calm, icy calm," I said desperately.

A shadow appeared in the doorway and a man's voice bellowed, "Found you!"

We all turned to see the Partner, his face contorted with hatred. He fired a gun at Saunders, but in his crazy excitement, he missed. Saunders ducked and swiveled and tried to pull a move on the Partner, but that guy knew his tricks. With punches and grunts, they fell out the door and continued to battle in the snow.

"Hurry, Albert," I urged.

Albert memoed an image of hearts cracking and shriveling and turning to dust. He couldn't keep sending the positive thoughts in the midst of this madness. The garage window told me all I needed to know; the red column was blasting up again and the spiders were roiling at the base like poison from a geyser.

Suddenly the Partner was back in the doorway, grinning like a lunatic. Had he killed Saunders? His eyes locked onto Albert and he smiled that angry smile. But Brit surprised the fiendish Partner, jumping him from behind, trying to grab his gun. Without mercy or remorse he smacked her head with his elbow—and she fell to the floor. Now the sick

Partner pointed his gun at Albert, and he fired. My brother slumped into the computer screen.

"Albert!" I cried.

But I didn't have time to help him because now the Partner was aiming at *me*.

36
Emergency

I dove behind the metal desk and when I peeked out, I was amazed to see that Lars was up and grabbing the guy's arm, trying to wrestle the gun from his hand. Neither of them saw Brit, who had recovered and was sneaking up behind them with a shovel. With a mighty whack, she hit the Partner and he fell—hitting his head a second time when he struck the concrete floor.

"Brit, he shot my Albert." I could hardly speak or think; the red spiders scuttled in a cloud around me. They were turning my snowy mind red, and my heart black. I barely noticed that Lars was checking Albert's pulse, listening for him to breathe. Lars was saying something but I couldn't hear him.

"What? What did you say?"

The red spiders told me that Albert was dead and the world was total crap.

Lars sounded muffled and far away. I strained to hear him. "He's alive, Mary."

"He's—alive?" I slogged back from the black and crammed my mind with snow.

"He's got a pulse and he's breathing." Poor Lars looked half-crazed himself with his bloodshot eyes and a greenish tinge to his skin. "Mary, we've got to finish this if we're going to save him—if we're going to save anything at all." Lars was speaking slowly in his effort to concentrate.

"None of us can think like Albert," Brit said. "He's the key—the Commodore said so."

I was so grateful that Albert still had a chance; that we all still had a chance. "Citizen Lady said *we all play a part*." I was trying to remember the exact words. "She said, 'Albert is the key, but Pearl is compassionate, Equationaut is clever, and Lars is brave. Excellent counterparts if one were to encounter an emergency.'"

"Yeah, I'd call this an emergency," Brit said.

"She also said Albert needed our support," Lars pointed out. "Maybe it wasn't enough to just *be* here. I mean, the blue light never turned on. Maybe Albert wasn't meant to do this alone."

"You're right." The soundness of what Lars said gave me hope.

"Albert had the key that opened the channel," Brit said. "Maybe we can do the rest."

"Quick, get the electrodes off Albert," I said. I was

walking a fine line of staying cold and calm but a small part of me dared to hope. "We'll hook ourselves up. Maybe we can bait the charge and do the commercial at the same time."

Brit and Lars started sticking the components on their heads anywhere they would adhere. I did the same.

"All the switches are on." I checked the window; it looked like the lasers were flashing. "I hope the tunnel is still open." We had to lean in toward each other because we were sharing the electrode gizmo. I held Brit's hand on one side, and Lars's hand on the other. For some reason I suddenly recalled the happy idea that had consoled me that morning—that maybe good thoughts made reality, too.

"Good thoughts make reality," I said excitedly, even as I tried to reel in my hope.

The pink light was back on, brighter than before.

"I think our good thoughts make reality," I said in a passion-filled voice. "Our good thoughts have value, and they're worth more than diamonds and gold."

I was speaking on the TV again, still on the big screen above Times Square, still standing in the snow doused in pink light—even though here I was, speaking these words from inside the garage. My eyes found Brit and we shared a

What the hay? moment. But I couldn't revel in the SMHRs's tricky technology. I had a memo to make.

"Our beautiful thoughts create beauty," I continued, "and our bad thoughts make things ugly. If we could all pretend for a minute that our good thoughts were golden and sparkly, maybe we could send them into the world and make it a better place. You could try. You could take your best thoughts and fill them up with love and kindness— because the world needs them right now."

I thought my deepest thoughts of love and concern, and the red spiders stayed away.

"You could call it a prayer or a wish or a dream. You could call it anything you want, but just think your best thoughts and fill them with love."

I quit holding hands with Brit and Lars and concentrated with all my might. I rolled my fingers into fists and squeezed my eyes shut.

"Try as hard as you can to bring all that love and kindness from your toes up to your heart, and zoom it into your arms." I raised my arms as high as they would go. "And then open your hands—" I stretched my fingers in the cold garage and I opened my eyes to see Brit and Lars with their arms raised, too. "AND THEN JUST LET IT ALL GO!"

I could imagine the love in my hands exploding like

fireworks, filling the garage, racing out the door, and shooting into the frosty sky.

When I checked the TV, everyone in Times Square was doing it. Everyone was raising their arms and sending their own versions of beauty and love into the world. Did they sense the critical moment, or were they just carried along with the crowd, like doing the wave with thousands of fans? It didn't matter. They all participated and smiled and laughed. They all shared their humanity and their joy.

To my astonishment, when those thousands of people opened their hands and let out their love—I could see it. It *was* as real as diamonds and gold. I could see the good explode and swirl like galaxies rushing into the atmosphere. And all those people could see it, too. They *oohed* and *ahhed* like they were watching fireworks, only the sparks and swirls and glittering lights came from each one of them.

If you could paint a picture of love, it would look like that night. The joyful faces and the eruptions of color and sparks and intertwining comets told a story of all that was good, all that was simple, and all that was kind. The worst of humanity might have been awful, but the very best was this heart-wrenching painting of love.

A blue light caught my eye. I gazed out the window to

see the thin blue beam stabbing at the heart of the red mist. It was the amplifier. At last!

There was a sound rising—maybe it was outside, or maybe it was inside my head. It reminded me of a train rumbling, coming from far, far away. By the sound and the feel of the vibration, it was coming closer. And it was big.

37
Back to the source

The rumble seemed to vibrate in my skull and was followed by a blast of energy that shook the forest. The sound shifted from a very low octave to an even lower-down bass—though I wasn't sure if it was a sound or a feeling—and then everything around us grew deadly quiet and still.

On the TV, I was saying *bring all the love and kindness* . . .

"And be super bold," I cut in. I smiled at Brit and Lars. What else could we do but hope and believe?

"The bait is working," Brit said. "I don't feel the red spiders at all."

"It's not over yet," Lars said cautiously. "Enough positive energy has to get into the half-constant to balance it out. Keep sending your best."

At this moment, I totally believed in the good. The belief gave me courage, and the courage gave me hope, and both those feelings gave me this sense of resolve, like it was set in cement—that somehow this world would be restored and I'd get my brother back. In my head I said, *Albie, if you are listening, Pearl will save you.*

We all held hands again. Lars kept his eyes on Brit, looking out for her like he always did. My eyes found my brother, and I thought about the monumental strength of loyalty.

"You guys are awesome." I said it like it was a casual thing, but only because I couldn't explain how big that feeling was.

In Times Square I was saying, "*Think your best thoughts and fill them with love...*"

The white lasers flashed and the blue beam burned, and the awful column of red mist that had been blasting into the sky made a total reversal. The woods trembled as the negative energy rolled in waves, faster and faster, like water circling a drain. It was a whirlpool of bad thoughts getting flushed through the channel that Albert had opened. It was *all* roaring back.

I cringed as a corner of the roof blew off in a quaking gust of red snow. Tree branches shook and cracked, and debris went flying as the thunderous, deafening train of bad thoughts rushed wildly back to the source. The garage rattled and convulsed and the glass in the window shattered. The forest quivered and leaned into the rip. I watched red mist fly off the Partner. It flew off of us, too. I felt thrilled with the triumph and could only imagine that sense of boundless joy being amplified exponentially. What power!

A bright light alerted us to the SMHR craft hovering low overhead, glowing like the sun. It was caught in the whirlpool and was getting sucked down. The craft tipped lower and lower, burning branches and cracking tree trunks, but the blue beam that amplified our thoughts kept shining—and then the whole craft disappeared, vanishing like poor Mr. Shinn at his last, crazy stand.

The idea came to me that this might have been intentional, that maybe the triad was so intrigued by the data they hoped to gain, they'd driven into the whirlpool on purpose. Either that, or they sacrificed themselves for our world—which filled me with an admiration that ached.

One last wave followed, but this one was bubbly and light. It was the same effervescence we'd felt on Mars, only now it had a purpose, a direction. Maybe it was the leftover good chasing the bad; maybe that's what Albert called good order. The brilliant wave bubbled and foamed like a stormy sea, pushing the red spiders back through the channel.

And then all was quiet.

Just quiet.

We were still holding hands, white-knuckled, gaping at each other when Albert raised his head, and blinked.

"Albert! Are you okay?"

A big bump was forming on his temple. It was a perfectly round welt that was bleeding. He groped around the desk and found something . . . he held out his hand and showed me the last electrode. It was a mess, with a bullet-size dimple in the center. I ran over and hugged him, and he let me.

"Albert, did it work?" I asked. "Did we close the rip?"

38
Good order day

The memo Albert sent was quietly triumphant. **Good Order Day**, it said. A follow-up memo showed a red spider content in a group of butterflies. The butterflies were flapping their wings, displaying pretty colors and patterns—when a door slammed shut on the memo and an oversized key locked it. The spiders and butterflies would stay where they belonged.

Pretty order, Albert emphasized, which made me think of the first message he'd ever sent me.

Lars was watching us. "What did he say?"

"He said it worked. The rip is closed."

"Where's Agent Saunders?" Brit asked nervously.

"I know where he is," a voice croaked from the floor. It was the horrible Partner trying to get up. "I almost killed him," he said. "I knocked him out when we were fighting—I almost shot him until I remembered . . . he owes me a coffee."

The Partner smiled through his pain and struggled to get up. Lars gave him a hand and the disheveled agent rose with a grunt. He limped outside to where Saunders was sprawled in the snow.

Poor Saunders. I hated to see his clean clothes all messed up. I knew he would have hated it, too.

I knelt down. "Agent Saunders?" I touched his face.

Behind me, the Partner said, "Terrence, how're you doing?"

"Your name is *Terrence*?" I couldn't keep the giggle from my voice.

His eyes opened and he groaned.

"That seems sort of funny," I said. "I mean, that your name is Terrence. It seems like kind of a fancy name for man as tough as you are."

He groaned again.

I held his hand and squeezed it. "You'll be okay, Saunders."

A BETI guy asked me to stand aside so he could treat his fellow agent, and I realized that our yard was alive with activity. The BETI forces were scurrying around and collecting the injured. Agent Saunders and the Partner were being helped into the woods. Helicopters were flying. They must have landed in Mr. Shinn's goat field—and now, they were exiting fast.

At the same time, emergency vehicles were cramming the cul-de-sac. There was an ambulance, a fire engine, and three police cars. I guess they'd come to investigate the "meth house" now that the BETI force gave them the okay. Their lights were flashing blue and red and white, and the uniformed people were rushing about—but I found it all strangely distant. I looked up. The moon was like a bright, fat nickel shining down. I could almost imagine a face on that nickel, and I was pretty sure it was smiling.

"Wow," said Brit. "This was an awesome sleepover. I think it was the best New Year's Eve we've ever had."

"I know!" I couldn't stop grinning and neither could Brit. We were pretty ecstatic about being alive.

"Brit, you look terrible," I said. She had a goose egg forming on her forehead where the Partner bashed her with his elbow.

"So do you," she said happily. "Lars got you good. You're going to have a black eye."

I felt my eye. It was sore and getting puffy. We *all* looked awful, with bumps and bruises from the fighting—and from the garage coming down around our ears! We began to limp over to the ambulance parked in the dead end. I hoped we could get cleaned up before Ma and Meemaw got home. Ma would have a heart attack seeing us like this, and Meemaw would probably start swearing at the EMTs. *"Hup to and get your rear in gear before these kids bleed out!*" I smirked to myself at the thought.

We tromped through the snow—which now had hundreds of footprints in it. The BETI force didn't have time to get those cleaned up. And yet, Agent Saunders, the Partner, and those faceless BETI guys were gone. In a few days when the snow melted, it would be like they'd never been.

Near the porch, Albert took my hand, which wasn't like him. The bump on his temple was even more swollen and it was turning purple. It was starting to make his eye bruised, too. Poor little guy.

He tugged on my jacket and I leaned down to check on him—maybe he felt sick.

He put his mouth by my ear and whispered in a voice that came from his throat, "I knew my Pearl would save me."

39
One week later . . .

Lars was going to drop Brit off at my house—we'd made a plan to study, which meant we'd probably just paint our nails and watch TV. Albert was on the couch, thinking about stuff. He never did start chattering away after he whispered in my ear. It was a gift for me, and I knew it. Maybe he'd talk more someday, and maybe he wouldn't. That was up to him.

We didn't know how to explain it all to Ma. It seemed so unlikely and crazy. But half the garage was gone, and our front door had bullet holes in it. Plus the four of us were pretty beat up—I still had a black eye, and Albert's head was swollen and bruised. So we told Ma and Meemaw *most* of the story—minus the information about the role Ma played in how Albert turned out. I didn't want her to know. I was sure she'd feel rotten and blame herself for participating in the one stupid experiment that changed Albert's life forever.

And anyhow, it was Albert's story to tell. When he wanted to talk to Ma about it, he would.

When Meemaw heard the bizarre tale, she took it well. She said, "I figured it was something like that."

What? How could she possibly? That made me laugh.

Agent Saunders talked to Ma on the phone and insisted that Albert get checked to make sure his head was okay. Saunders said the "Bureau" would cover it, as well as medical visits for the Stickles. Plus there'd be money for the damage done to our property from some "federal claim group." Saunders was all official about the deal, so Ma had to accept the incredible story.

The weirdest thing was that nobody (not even Ma or Meemaw) recognized me as the girl in the commercial. Albert memoed me that the SMHR units had an app or something that altered the sound and the picture. They'd done it this way because I guess they picked up on how I wouldn't like the attention, which was true. I was grateful. The SMHR units saved me from being pestered by tons and tons of people. Pretty thoughtful, for machines.

Most of the world thought it was just a show or a stunt—and the triad was so smooth there was no way to trace it to them. The mass hysteria and the violence that occurred beforehand couldn't be explained. It was chalked up to just that—mass hysteria; a viral blip of madness that happened one shameful New Year's Eve.

And the amazing fireworks of good thoughts that followed? Well, that couldn't be explained either. I had to admit that the fireworks could have been another trick of the SMHRs's technology, but I liked to believe it was the people who did it—just regular people creating something beautiful in a moment of goodness and unity. Those who were there and who experienced it said that they felt wonderful. They said the wonderful feeling lasted for a long, long time. I could still feel it, that sense of joy and wonder. But I guess I felt like that a lot of the time anyway, which was a super nice way to feel.

Most of the snow had melted, and with it, the evidence that we'd waged a battle here at the end of Myrtle Road. All that was left was a shrinking snowman that Brit and I had made the day after. We'd dressed him in an old trench coat and put dark glasses on him and called him Agent Saunders. Later we added a red plastic squirt gun and a broken earmuff that was supposed to be his communication device. The *fun-relativity factor* was still working because we definitely got some good giggles out of making that dumb snowman.

I went out to meet Brit by the road. She was climbing out of Lars's truck just as a black car pulled up behind them.

It was the real Agent Saunders.

He got out of his car and gave us a curt nod. His overcoat was crisp and his suit was impeccable, but his handsome face was definitely worse for wear after the beating he'd taken from the Partner.

"I wanted to check on you kids in person," he said, very proper and businesslike. "Agent Guy couldn't be here; he's still in the hospital with a concussion."

Brit grimaced.

"He'll be fine," Saunders said quickly. "He's getting tip-top care."

"I was sorta worried," Brit confided.

"I'm glad to see the four of you are recovering. I brought some compensation for your mom, and for the Stickle family." He patted some envelopes in his pocket. "The Bureau's going to pay for medical expenses plus damages."

"The Bureau, huh? That's pretty nice," Brit said. "Thanks, Saunders. Hey, could I get, like, a whole check-up and some prescriptions if I needed them?"

I knew what Brit was thinking—something for her skin!

"I would expect nothing less," he assured her.

"How are *you* feeling, Saunders?" I asked.

"Excellent."

He said this like, *why wouldn't I be excellent?* Then he furtively glanced left and right. "I have something I want you to see." He made a curt nod to the briefcase he was carrying.

"Well, come on in. I know how to make coffee—oh wait, you don't like coffee."

Lars came in, too, and after an awkward pause in the front room, Lars said, "Agent Saunders, I wanted to thank you for knocking me out when you did. I was losing it." He held out his hand for Saunders to shake.

"It was hell," Saunders said. He clutched Lars's hand and shook it. "I don't know how you did what you did, Lars. Even from where I was standing, I could barely hang on to my sanity." Saunders gave Lars a formal nod, like he'd won an award or something. Lars blushed pink but he stood straighter.

"Ma is still at work," I said. "And Meemaw is at Mrs. Zucker's. Sorry you can't meet them." Secretly, I could picture Meemaw commenting about Saunders looking uptight—or she might pop off about a stick being up his you-know-what. So I guess I was relieved she wasn't here.

"Actually, I *knew* your mother and grandmother wouldn't be at home." (Saunders just couldn't resist the chance to be a know-it-all.)

Brit arched her eyebrows but didn't say anything.

Saunders promptly set his briefcase on the dining room table and opened it. He pulled out a laptop and opened that, too. Then he navigated to a file he'd saved. Once again he looked around cautiously as if he had something to hide. The four of us gathered around him as he clicked PLAY on the screen.

40
Classified

The screen showed the big control room at NASA where the tech crew was getting the latest feed from the Rover. The camera scanned the rocky landscape, and then it focused in on three shapes in the distance.

Saunders turned to us and gave us his uptight little grin. Then he watched the screen again—so we did, too.

The camera panned closer and closer to reveal three humanoid figures standing on the rocky plane. They were lined up tall to short, dressed in black, smiling. They began to wave a childish, four-fingered wave.

At the bottom of the NASA screen was a strip for a crawler-message. And these words were rolling by:

This reality is a conscious, real-time event..........It has no distortions or other possibilities..........It could only

```
happen this way, and in fact, it always
happened  this  way.............In  short,
Operation Super Bold was a success.....FYI,
Lambert was meant for the exemplary one,
Pearl.....................................
..........................................
..........................................
........................Goodbye
```

We all exchanged stunned glances—except for Saunders, who was smirking and shaking his head. He was getting a real kick out of how cheeky the SMHR units were, but the mention of Lambert sorta made me want to cry. It shined a whole new light on how things began with me and Albert and how thoughtful the SMHR units had been. I was so glad to see they survived their journey—and they probably got tons of data.

Brit spoke first. "Thanks, Saunders. Thank you for showing us this. I feel a lot better knowing they made it."

"Agent Saunders, is showing us this video going to get you in trouble?" Lars asked. "I mean wouldn't this information be classified?"

Saunders seemed to appreciate Lars's concern. "After everything you kids went through, we figured we owed you.

Agent Guy and I were extremely careful in appropriating this file. No one's going to know about this but us."

Albert sent me a memo that had cartoon binoculars with "BETI" stamped on the side. They were focusing in on four dumb-looking stick drawings. Under each figure blinked a name—Albert, Mary, Brit, and Lars.

"Hmm," I said quizzically, "will you be keeping an eye on us, Saunders?"

Surprise and irritation flashed before he could hide it. Then he sort of snickered. "For some reason, you four seem to attract very unusual phenomenon. The Bureau is—shall we say—*interested*." He'd gone back to being the aloof and braggy Saunders. "Don't concern yourselves. BETI is, above all things, discreet."

Suddenly Albert straightened up to face Agent Saunders. He held out his hand to the tall man, mimicking what he'd seen Lars do. Saunders seemed baffled for a moment, but then he grasped the little hand and they solemnly shook on a deal that perhaps only Albert understood.

That's when Albert sent me a memo that felt safe and secure, the way I feel in our little house with Ma in the kitchen, and Meemaw folding clothes, and Albert counting dust in the dining room, and Brit raising her eyebrows at me, and Lars pointing at Brit to show her that he is always on her side. In the midst of all these comforting bits was the image of a single black shoe. The shoe had integrity; it was trustworthy, and above all, courageous.

I looked at Albert—and then at Agent Saunders. "You're a good man, Saunders." I patted his arm. "I'm glad it's you. Maybe we'll see you around."

"You certainly will not," he snapped, like I'd offended him.

"Oh, brother." Brit rolled her eyes.

At that moment, something small but really big happened. With a contagious tickle, sort of like a SMHR unit, Albert laughed.